"We're All Mad Here"

-

A novel by

RJ Niemczura

In loving memory of Bowen Wilcox

CHAPTER ONE: The Search for Tomorrow

I've never been a big fan of my family.

That may sound like a horrible thing to say, though I assure you that if you knew my family, you'd agree. They have always left much to be desired. There were no family dinners. There were no vacations. Talking about your feelings was reserved for sessions with your therapist. If you didn't want to talk to her, well, you were fucked. I've never understood the concept that just because you share a drop of blood with someone, that they're supposed to be on the receiving end of your undying love. I've always thought that love was something you had to *earn.*

I guess I'm a hypocrite, though, because here I am. Alone. Unemployed, with no money and nowhere to live. I hailed a taxi from the corner outside my favorite Chinese restaurant. When the ugly yellow car pulled to the curb, I fumbled into the back seat and handed the driver a crumpled up piece of paper with an address scribbled across it. "Upper east side?" He asked, surprised.

"My sister's house." I mumbled.

I wish I could say that this trip to my sisters house was rooted in a loving desire to fix our relationship, that I had friends lining up offering me a place to stay. As it turns out, however, your "friends" are only interested in you when you come with an affluent lifestyle attached. When you're down and out, you're alone.

As I sat in the back of the cab, I found myself staring at the window. Not out of the window. Not through the window, but at it. I watched as tiny raindrops beaded up at the top of the glass, slowly making their way to the bottom, where they collapsed in a small puddle in the space between the door and the window.

Rain falls, these raindrops fulfill their purpose, evaporate back into the sky somewhere, just to do it all again. If they don't like where they've landed the first time, they'll get a second chance. A third, a fourth, a fifth. I couldn't help to feel that there was no second chance for me. I don't like where I've landed, yet there's no magical force waiting to evaporate me back into the atmosphere. There's no thundercloud out there waiting to drop me out of the sky and into a better life.

My life is less significant than a fucking raindrop.

As the taxi made it's way through the streets of Manhattan, I reminisced about the great things this city was supposed to bring me. The fame, the fortune, the lifestyle. I had everything I had ever dreamed of, yet here I was with nothing at all, with nothing left but the memory of a lifestyle I was never meant to live, a career that I was never destined to succeed at. Yet, I had just as much as I'd ever had. There was never anything more to my life. There's something to be said about having everything, and nothing.

As the cab pulled up to the curb outside my sister's brownstone, I fumbled for my wallet. Pulling out my American Express card, I swiped it through the reader and grabbed my bag. As I slid across the backseat to open the door, the taxi driver spoke for the first time since we had left Brooklyn. "Sir" he said. "Your card has been declined."

I felt my cheeks get hot. I choked back the lump in my throat and reached for my wallet once more. I pulled out two crumpled up 20-dollar bills and handed to them, avoiding eye contact. "Keep the change." I said.

The cab pulled off and I turned to make my way through the gate and up to the front door. I reached for the buzzer, but before I could press it, the door swung open. There stood a tall, blonde-haired teenage boy. We stared at each other for a moment, before he finally spoke: "Can I help you?" he asked.

"Yes." I mumbled, still choking back tears. "I'm here to see Valerie."

"May I ask who you are?" he replied.

"I think..." I started. "I think I'm your uncle."

He looked at me for a long moment, before moving down the steps. He grabbed my bag, and motioned for me to follow him inside. We entered into a grand, marble foyer. "You're Austin, aren't you?" I asked. He nodded. "I haven't seen you since you were a little boy."

He didn't reply, but instead motioned for me to follow him once more. We entered the living room, which was decorated lavishly in various shades of white and beige. This was most assuredly Valerie's house. She lived life as if the Kennedys were going to pop in for tea at any moment.

Austin told me to wait there as he went to retrieve his mother. As I sat alone in the room, I glanced at the fireplace mantle. Pictures of Valerie, her husband Charles, and their two children cluttered the length of the mantle. Even Charles' siblings snagged a spot. But there were no pictures of our mother, and there were no pictures of me.

Finally, I heard the click of stiletto heels against the marble tile in the foyer. Seconds later, Valerie appeared in the living room door.

"What the hell are you doing here?" She asked, coldly.

"I..." I started. "I need a place to stay."

"Well, you certainly can't stay here." She hissed.

"Valerie, I'm your brother." I said. The hypocrisy in my own words made me cringe.

"And when was the last time I heard from you?" She asked. If I didn't know better, I would've sworn that her voice had cracked a little.

"I know." I said. "But I need you now. Please."

She didn't say anything at first. Instead, she moved to the opposite side of the room. She grabbed the decanter of vodka from the mahogany sidebar, and began pouring the liquid into a small crystal glass. She took several sips as she stood gazing out the window, her back to me. There were tears in her eyes as she finally turned to face me, splashing her drink in my face.

I didn't say a word.

"I can't deal with this right now. I can't deal with *you* right now. " She said. "I'll have Austin put your bags in the guest room. Don't get comfortable. I'll deal with you tomorrow." With that, she strode straight past me and out of the living room. A moment later, I heard the front door close behind her.

Austin showed me to the guest room and asked me if I needed anything. I told him I was fine, thanking him as he left the room. As he closed the door behind him, I made my way across the room, to the wooden desk near the window. I opened the top drawer, removed a pen and tablet, and scribbled a note.

> "Dear Valerie,
> I love you. Please forgive me.
> -Jackson"

I left the note on the desk as I grabbed my bag and dumped its contents out onto the plush comforter covering the bed. I sorted through the mess of clothes and accessories until I found what I was looking for.

With my left hand, I unscrewed the white lid from the orange bottle. I dumped the entire bottle of pills into my hand, grabbed the water bottle Austin had left for me, and with one swig, I swallowed them all. I sat down at the edge of the bed for a moment, as I began to cry. Several moments later, I pushed myself up onto the bed completely.

My final selfish act. In my sister's house, and I decided to die.

CHAPTER TWO: Days of Our Lives

I opened my eyes slowly, though they felt as if they'd been stuffed with cotton. I blinked repeatedly, as the ceiling above me came into focus. The ugly rectangular ceiling panels became clearer, sterile white plastered with flecks of gray. For a moment, I couldn't move. Where was I?

I inhaled deeply, and just as quickly as the smell of the room filled my nostrils, the sinking realization of where I was set in. I knew this smell, I'd been here before. I was in the hospital.

Fuck. I lived.

Before I had time to further process this disappointment, the door to my room swung open. There stood Austin, my 16-year-old nephew. His blonde hair was messy and unkempt, his shirt untucked from his sweatpants. For a moment, we stared at each other, neither of us saying a word. And then I noticed. He was blinking back tears. He moved towards me and began to speak.

"I was worried about you." He said.

"Why?" I asked. "You don't know me." He didn't say anything, and I could tell that my words had hurt him. "I'm sorry." I mumbled. "I didn't mean to be rude."

"It's okay." He replied.

"Usually there's nobody here." I said.

"This has…" He paused. "This has happened before?"

"Maybe a time or two." I said, with a laugh. Before I finished speaking, he turned his back to me.

"It's not funny. You could have died."

"That was kind of the point." I shot back. Why did he care so much? Why was he even here?

"I'm sorry." I said, sarcastically. "But if a man can't joke about his own attempted suicide, what can he joke about?"

He didn't answer. Instead, he made his way to the opposite side of the room. He stood there, his back still to me, as he pretended to examine the ugly floral painting that hung against the stark white wall. Eventually, he turned towards me once more, grabbing the small chair behind him and pulling it to my bedside. He sat down next to me, looking me directly in the eye.

"Why'd you do it?" He asked.

"I don't know." I said. "It seemed like the best option, in that moment. I don't know how to explain it to you."

"You honestly wanted to die?" He asked.

"Yes."

He looked away.

"It was horrible." He said.

"What was?" I asked.

"Finding you, like that". He said, his voice cracking.

I had never even considered the fact that Austin might be the one to find me. Typical.

"I thought you were dead." He continued. "I walked in and you were lying there and at first I thought you were sleeping.'

He paused for a moment.

"But then I saw the empty pill bottle on the floor, and the note. And I knew. I knew what you had done, but I panicked. I didn't know what to do."

"I'm sorry, Austin." I said. "I shouldn't have put you in that position. I shouldn't have dragged you into my fucked up situation, and I'm sorry. Really."

"I tried to take your pulse, and I couldn't find it." He paused again. "I really thought you were dead." I didn't reply. I couldn't look at him. After a moment, he continued.

"I didn't call 911 right away." He said.

"What?" I asked, confused.

"For a second..."He paused. "For a second, I thought...You know, that's what you wanted. You wanted to die, obviously. Who was I to fuck that up? But I just couldn't do it. I couldn't just let you die." My heart sank as the realization set in. Before I could stop myself, the words came out of my mouth.

"You've thought about it too." I said. "You've thought about killing yourself before."
He looked up from his lap, startled." What did you just say?" He asked. His voice was angry, but his eyes were scared.

"Only somebody who's thought about killing themselves would think like that." I said. "Only someone who's been there would understand." He looked at me for a moment, before grabbing his coat and standing from the chair. As he began to move towards the door, he spoke. "You don't know what you're talking about.

"I didn't mean to offend you." I said. He stopped walking, just as he reached the door. "I love you." I said, softly.

What was happening to me?

"I do. I wouldn't say that if I didn't mean it. You are my family and, I know I've never been very good at that. I do care about you, though. And I know you don't know me, but if you need anything, I'm here. I'm here."

He didn't say a word. Instead, he moved towards me. When he reached the side of the bed, he leaned down and kissed my forehead. He looked down at me, blinking back tears, and squeezed my hand.

The next few days in the hospital passed without much incident. I was being kept on suicide watch, which meant no showering alone, no sharp objects in the room, no shoelaces, and most of all, no fucking privacy. I suppose they expected me to feel lucky that I even got to keep the goddamn bed sheets. This morning, I was awoken by my night nurse, Anne, just as her shift was coming to an end.

"Mr. Arrington" She cooed, softly, as if she hadn't just deliberately woken me up. "You are being discharged today. Your morning nurse should be in within the hour with paperwork for you."

"Thank you." I mumbled. You'd think I'd be excited to leave. You'd think I'd be excited to go home. But what did that even mean for me? Anne began to exit the room, but just as she reached the door, she turned around and began to speak once more.

"I almost forgot!" She said, reaching into her pocket. "Your sister left this. She said to have you call when you're ready to be picked up." She extended her arm towards me, and sure enough, clutched in her palm was a small piece of paper with a phone number scribbled across it.

"My sister?" I asked.

"Yes...I believe she said her name was Valerie." Anne said. "Is that not correct?"

"No, no. It is." I replied. "I'm just surprised to hear that she would do this. She hasn't been to see me. I don't blame her, though. Not really." Anne paused for a moment.

"For what it's worth, she did call to check on you." And with that, she left.

After a few moments I decided to get out of bed and move myself to the ugly, uncomfortable plastic chair near the window. I gazed out over the busy Manhattan landscape, and I began to take notice of the people wandering the streets below. What were they thinking? Where were they going? How many of them also wanted to die? Before I knew it, I was asleep.

I dreamt of the raindrops from the day before. I dreamt that there was some mystical force that could suck me up and drop me into a new reality - one much more pleasant than my own. I dreamt of my mother. I dreamt of all the things we should have done together. All the things we never did.

I was awakened by the sound of my morning nurse, Julianne, entering the room. Julianne had been my nurse every morning, and she was my favorite.

"Good morning, Jackson!" She said, smiling and much too cheery for this time of morning.

"Good morning, Jules." I said. I had taken the liberty of giving her a nickname in the three days I had known her. She had been assigned to make sure I didn't kill myself in the shower each morning, which will quickly bond you to someone.

"I have your discharge papers." She said, handing me a clipboard with several papers underneath the clasp.

I scribbled my signature onto the pages and stood from the chair, making my way to the bedside table where Julianne had placed my clothes upon entering the room. I reached behind my neck and undid the drawstring on my hospital gown, letting it fall to the floor. Julianne averted her eyes. As I began getting dressed, she started to speak once more.

"I don't usually do this." She said. "It's probably not appropriate, but..." She placed a small piece of paper on the bed, and written on it was her phone number.

"Are you hitting on me?" I asked.

"Absolutely not!" She said, half laughingly. "Look. This may be completely out of line, but I hear things. Nurses hear things, like the conversation you had with your nephew. I heard the things you said in your sleep. I just thought, maybe you could use a friend." I looked at her for a moment. "What makes you think I don't have friends?" I asked.

"I'm sure you do." She said. "I just thought maybe you might want to talk to someone who's been where you are." Our eyes locked for a moment, as I began to process what she was saying. "Just a thought, really." She said, moving towards the door. "Good luck, Jackson."

As she closed the door behind her, I moved towards the phone that hung from the wall next to the bed, fumbling for the paper Anne had given me earlier. Finding it in my pocket, I unfolded it and punched the numbers into the receiver. A man with a deep voice answered the phone; somehow knowing who I was before I even spoke.

The scenario unfolded exactly as I would've expected. The driver pulled the black town car up to the entrance of the hospital and stood outside of it, waiting for me to get in, much like the past, when I had a career. Except that this time there was no joy involved, nobody waiting for me with bated breath. To be honest, I wasn't sure if there was anyone waiting for me at all. The feelings were shockingly similar.

The driver didn't ask me where I wanted to go, and I half assumed he was taking me to a halfway house, if not the bus station. I sat in the backseat in complete silence, wondering what would happen when I got back to the house, if that was, in fact, where we were going. I worried what Valerie would say. I worried for Austin.

We pulled up to the house and, just as expected, the driver hopped out of the car and opened my door for me. I stood from the car and blinked rapidly as my eyes adjusted to the bright sunlight that had somehow managed to fill the sky in the short trip from the hospital. I thanked him for driving me. He nodded and was on his way.

I made my way to the gate and, to my surprise, found that the front door was unlocked. I entered the foyer and called out. "Val?" I didn't get a response. I made my way into the living room. From there, I could here Valerie and her husband Charles talking behind the semi-closed door of the nearby den. "He cannot stay here!" Charles spat, angrily.

"Charles, he's my brother!" Valerie pleaded.

"And since when has that mattered to you?"

"We may not have a great relationship, but he is my family and he is obviously in trouble. He's not well, Charles." Valerie said, her voice quivering slightly.

"I don't give a fuck! He will not stay in my house!" He shouted back at her. I turned to leave. As I made my way through the living room, I stopped at the sidebar. I stared at the crystal decanter of vodka in front of me and, after a moment, I took it in my hand. Making my way through the living room, I could almost swear I heard the sound of a slap come from the den.

I made my way upstairs and quietly shut the door to the guest room behind me. I entered the bathroom, setting the vodka on the counter as I shut the door. I removed my clothes slowly, as I felt the lump in my throat rising. Standing there in nothing but my underwear, I stared at myself in the mirror. I examined my almost naked body as if it were something completely foreign to me. I ran my fingers along the various scars that marked me, my battle wounds of sorts.

I moved forward, towards the vanity. Approaching the mirror, I touched my right hand to my face, something that I no longer recognized. My cheeks, once rosy and full of life, now lay concave and grey. I reached for the bottle of vodka.

I grabbed the cup from next to the sink and began filling it with the clear liquid, splashing some onto the counter as my hand shook. Slowly, I took a sip. As I lowered the cup from my lips, I caught my own eyes in the mirror. I stared back at myself, into my own eyes. I saw nothing.

I felt the glass break in my hand. Looking down, I saw the blood covering the shattered pieces of glass that remained clasped in my palm. I didn't feel it. I didn't feel anything. I dropped to my knees, feeling nothing as they banged against the cold, tile floor. Before I could stop myself, I was lying on the ground, in tears.

Several moments later, the door to the bathroom opened. I locked eyes with my sister, but neither of us spoke. She moved towards me, dropping to her knees besides me. After a moment, she laid down next to me, placing her head near mine. I could feel the uneven rise and fall of her chest as she cried.

When I woke up, there was a pillow under my head and a blanket draped over my body. The mess of blood and glass had been cleaned. I stood up, looking at my hand for a moment before the pain set in. I rinsed the wounds under hot water for several seconds, before wrapping my hand in a towel and moving towards the bedroom.

Upon entering the bedroom, I could hear the sounds of an argument coming from downstairs. I made my way to the door and realized that it was not Charles that Valerie was arguing with this time. It was a female voice – one that I recognized.

I opened the door slowly and made my way to the top of the stairs. Hair perfectly coifed, she stood at the bottom of the staircase in a blood red dress and matching stiletto heels.

My mother.

"What are you doing here?" I asked.

"If my son can come here to die, I thought the least I could do was join him."

CHAPTER THREE: The Edge of Night

I made my way slowly down the steps, feeling as cold beads of sweat formed on my forehead. "What did you say?" She looked at me for a moment before she spoke. "I think you heard me."

"I see you're just as insensitive as ever." Valerie chimed in.

I had finally reached the bottom of the steps. I stood for a moment, still in shock, as I stared at my mother. She breezed swiftly past me, however, as she made her way through the foyer. "Oh, *please.*" She cooed as she entered the living room. "You are much too sensitive."

"Mother." Valerie said, following slowly behind her. "Your son just tried to kill himself, and you're here to make jokes about it?"

"Who's joking, Valerie?" She replied, coldly.

I followed them into the living room, slowly. As I entered the room, I made my way to the sidebar near the bay window. "Still drinking?" My other asked, sarcastically. "Mother!" Valerie shouted. "What is wrong with you? Do you have any idea what Jackson must be feeling right now?"

Our mother paused for a moment, looking Valerie up and down slowly. She smiled slyly and turned towards me. "Do you have any idea how *I* felt, to have learned about my own son's attempted suicide on the internet?" She snarled, articulating each letter word, maliciously.

I swallowed the lump in my throat. Even now, as a grown adult, I was scared of this woman. Yet at the forefront of my mind was a thought of relief, that my attempted suicide would even be relevant enough for her to have heard online. How sad.

"I didn't..." I began. "I didn't think you'd..."

"Care?!" She snapped back, cutting me off. "You didn't think I'd care that you had tried to *kill* yourself?" I didn't reply. After a moment, she continued. "Well, you're right." She said. " I don't."

"What the fuck is *wrong* with you?" Valerie spat, angrily.

Before I had a chance to process what she had said, our mother stood from the couch. She moved quickly towards Valerie, stopping just inches away from her. She stood like this for several seconds, staring coldly into Valerie's eyes, before raising her right arm and slapping my sister across the face. "I am your mother." She snarled, angrily. "You will not speak to me like that." Valerie stood still for a moment, her hand clasping the red mark our mother had left on her cheek. "What is wrong with you?" She whispered, her voice cracking.

"And you see..." Our mother began. "This is why I don't give a damn. About either of you! Everything with the two of you has always been my fault. At what point will you grow up and take responsibility for your actions? Why don't you take a look at your goddamn selves? You're no angels."

"And how were we ever supposed to be?" I shot back at her, finding my voice for the first time since she had arrived. "You didn't raise us to be anything but selfish, just like you."

"You are a 26 year old man." She said. "It's about time you owned your own behavior. You haven't lived in my home, under my influence, in *years.* The fuck up you've become? That's not on me, dear, that's all on you."

"So let me get this straight." I replied. "You found out that I tried to take my own life, and you came here to mock me? To avoid taking any responsibility for the awful mother you've been to me, and to Valerie for that matter?"

"I came here because momentarily, stupidly, I gave a fuck." She spat. "But I knew the moment I laid eyes on you, on the both of you, that you were still nothing more than the entitled brats you've always been."

"Then feel free to leave." I said. "Nobody here needs you."

"Really?" She asked, sarcastically. "So how's your life going without me?" I felt my face grow hot, the lump in my throat growing once more. Before I had a chance to reply, Valerie spoke. "It's time for you to go." She hissed. Our mother opened her mouth to speak once more, but Valerie cut her off before she had the chance. "Now."

She looked at her for a moment, before turning to leave. She made her way out of the living room and through the foyer. As she reached the front door, she turned and spoke once more. "This conversation isn't over." She said. "Try not to off yourselves before I get back."

For what seemed like hours, Valerie and I stood in silence, before she finally spoke.
"I'm sorry you had to deal with that." She said. "It's okay." I replied. "I'm used to her."
I glanced towards Valerie for the first time since our mother had left, and I noticed that she was crying. "Valerie…" I started.

"I can't do this." She said, cutting me off. "Okay…"I said. "But we do have a lot to talk about."

"I know." She said. "But I'm already late to pick up Madeleine. I don't have time to think about that woman." Before I could reply, she turned and started to leave the room. As she reached the doorway, she turned around and faced me once more. We locked eyes for a moment, before she moved towards me again, wrapping her arms around me and embracing me in a hug. "I love you, too." She whispered to me.

After a moment, she unwrapped her arms from around my shoulders and turned to leave the room. Just then, I noticed for the first time a small scratch under her eye, and three, small, finger-shaped bruises around her wrist. Before I could say anything, she was gone.

I made my way out of the living room and up the grand staircase. Instead of taking the first right, into my room, I made my way to the end of the hall. I raised my hand and knocked three times on Austin's door. "Hold on!" He shouted. I could hear him scrambling to put something away. After several seconds, the door swung open. And I could smell it. "Really?" I asked. "Are you getting high right now?" His face was frozen, a panicked look in his eyes.

"What? Do you think I'm going to tell on you?" I replied, laughing, as I entered the room. He quickly shut the door behind me, shuffling awkwardly and saying nothing.
"I wasn't…" He said, nervously. "I don't know what you're talking about." I laughed again. "You're never going to fool me, Austin." I said. "Not when it comes to things like this."

"So are you going to tell my mother?" He asked.

"Of course not." I replied. "But I am going to ask for a hit." He looked at me, wide eyed for a moment. Finally, he nodded towards a desk in front of the window. I made my way over to it and pulled open the top drawer to find a fully packed, beautiful glass bowl. I lit it, inhaling deeply before exhaling the cloud of smoke in the direction of the window.

"Relax." I said. "Sit down, tell me what you're going through." I took a seat on the edge of his bed and motioned for him to do the same. "I'm not going through anything!" He snapped, not moving.

"Look." I said. "I didn't mean to ambush you the other day. Or now, for that matter. I do recognize that tone in your voice, though, the look in your eyes, your thought process. You're going through something, and I just want you to know that I'd like to be here for you." He didn't reply for a moment. He turned away from me, wiping his eyes. "I don't even know you." He said, his voice frail.

"I know." I said. "But I'd like to change that."

"I don't need anyone else in my life. I have plenty of friends." He replied. "Really?" I said, moving towards him. "Because it's a Friday night, and you're alone in your room smoking pot. I'd bet most kids your age are out doing something a little more exciting right now." He turned to face me once more. "So what are you, making fun of me now?"

"Of course not." I replied. "You didn't exactly see a flock of people rushing to check on me in the hospital, did you?"

He didn't reply.

"I don't want you to end up like me, Austin. I see myself in you. But you can do so much more."

"Why should I trust you?"

"Because I am your family." I replied.

"That doesn't mean much, obviously." He began. "You're my mother's family too and it's been how many years since I even saw you last?"

"You're right."

"I don't know if I can just trust you like that." He replied, without making eye contact.

"Tomorrow afternoon." I said. "Let me take you somewhere. There's something I want to show you." He hesitated for a moment. "Okay." He replied, finally. I moved across the room, towards the door.

"Next time you're going to smoke in here, at least put a towel in front of the door." I heard him laugh as I closed the door behind me. I made my way down the hall and into my room, throwing myself onto my bed and falling asleep, fully dressed.

I woke up to the sound of a loud thud from downstairs. I rolled over and looked at the alarm clock on my bedside table.

3:09 A.M.

For a moment, I sat in bed, silently. Then it happened again, the sound of something moving downstairs. I stood from my bed, making my way towards the door. I cracked it open slightly, and after several seconds, I heard the noise once more.

I opened the door completely and moved through the doorway and towards the staircase. I tiptoed down the stairs as quietly as possible and, as I reached the bottom step, I heard something moving in the living room.

I crept across the foyer, making my way to the entryway of the living room. There she was, once again. This time, she was sitting. In a long, chiffon nightgown, mother sat on Valerie's couch. A martini in one hand, lit cigarette in the other, a silk scarf wrapped tightly around her head.

After a moment, she noticed me standing in the doorway. She looked at me, blankly, for several seconds, her eyes puffy and red, almost as if she'd been crying.

"I suppose now's as good a time as any to tell you that you're not really my son."

CHAPTER FOUR: The Young & the Restless

"Excuse me?" I said, moving closer to her. "You heard me." She said, dryly. I continued moving towards her. As I reached the edge of the couch where she sat, staring at me coldly as she took a drag of her cigarette.

I paused for a moment, before moving towards the opposite side of the room. Suddenly, I found myself choking back tears as I stared out the window. "What, nothing to say?" She asked, with a chuckle.

I didn't respond to her question, as I reached for the decanter of vodka once more. Grabbing a crystal glass from the shining silver platter at the end of the sidebar, I poured the drink, raising the cool glass to my mouth, wincing slightly as the vodka stung my lips. Finally, I turned around to face my mother once more.

"What the fuck are you talking about?" My voice was quiet, but filled with rage.
She smiled. "Did you honestly think…" She paused, taking a sip of her drink. "That someone like *me* could have given birth to someone like *you?*" I didn't say a word. She stared at me for a long moment, before continuing.

"What is it you want from me? From this?" I spat.

"You spent your whole life resenting me." She said, her voice quivering slightly. "You resented me because I wasn't the mother you wanted. And now you know."

"I don't understand." I said. The room began to feel as if it were spinning. She stood from the couch, setting her glass on the end table next to her. She took one last puff of her cigarette, dropping the butt into her half-full martini glass, she moved across the room, towards me, beginning to speak once more. "I'm afraid I don't understand your confusion, dear."

"So my whole life…" I began, but she cut me off. "You spent your whole life crying because I wasn't a good enough mother! And now you know why. Even though I found it in the goodness of my heart to take you in, you've never appreciated me." She paused, as she raised her hand to my cheek. She caressed her fingers along the side of my face, before she continued.

"What did you turn out to be?" She whispered, harshly. "A disappointment. A failure." I turned to pour myself another drink. "Sure." She said, the smile etching itself across her face again. "Drink your problems away. It's worked so well for you in the past."

"Shut UP!" I screamed, loudly, throwing the glass across the room. It crashed into the large glass fireplace, smashing into thousands of tiny, broken pieces. After several seconds, I heard as Valerie's bedroom door swung open, quickly. We stood in silence as the sound of footsteps drew nearer and nearer. Before long, Valerie stormed into the room, quickly fumbling to turn on the bright overhead light. "What the *hell* is going on in here?!" She asked, incredulously, as she observed the state of the room.

"Mom?" She continued, surprise and confusion spreading rapidly across her face. "What are you doing here? You're going to wake Austin and Madeleine. Neither of us responded. The look of horror on her face slowly turned to one of compassion as she looked repeatedly from our mother to me. Eventually, she turned towards our mother. "What did you do?" She hissed.

"Apparently..." I began, cutting her off before she could start speaking. "This witch isn't my mother." Neither of them replied. "Go on!" I hissed, angrily. "Tell her, Tabitha! That *is* what I'm supposed to call you, isn't it? You're not my mother, but we're on a first name basis at least, right?" I paused, before continuing angrily. "Tell her! Tell Valerie what you told me." She looked at me, devilishly, for a moment, before speaking. "This news is of no surprise to your sister." She cooed.

A look of horror spread across Valerie's face as tears welled up in her eyes. "What is that supposed to mean?" I asked, my voice cracking.

"Your sister, Saint Valerie, knows." She said. "She's known for years." I couldn't speak. I stared at Valerie, in shock. She wiped tears away from her eyes, yet I felt nothing but the lump forming in the back of my throat. "Is that true?" I asked, softly. "Yes." She said, her voice shaking as she swallowed her tears.

"How long?" I asked.

"Jackson, I didn't..." She began.

"How fucking LONG, Valerie?" I shouted. "How long have you known this?"

"Ten years." She replied.

"Ten years? Ten fucking YEARS?" I shouted, my hands shaking uncontrollably as I raised them to cover my face. "I'm so sorry." She said, softly.

"How did you find out?" I asked, coldly.

"I was at the old house, in Maine." She began. She paused to wipe the tears from her face. "I was in the attic looking for old pictures, for some kind of stupid project Austin was doing for school I stumbled across a letter."

"What kind of letter?" I asked.

Before Valerie could reply, Tabitha spoke out, angrily. "A letter between your father and his whore."

"My mother." I said, though the words didn't truly register with me.

"If you want to call a woman who was willing to trade her kid for a hundred thousand bucks and a plane ticket out of town "your mother", then yes." Tabitha replied, laughing. "Your mother."

I started to move towards her, quickly, as the rage consumed me entirely. Valerie moved between us, quickly, as she grabbed my face and forced me to look her in the eye. "I'm so sorry, Jackson." She said, as she lowered her hands from my face. "I wanted to tell you. But she convinced me that it would only hurt you more."

"Hurt me more than finding out you BOTH lied to me?" I shouted.

"You had just gotten out of rehab, Jackson. You were finally clean. For the first time. I was worried that you would fall off the wagon. She told me you would. And, at the time, I was stupid enough to believe she cared. I should've known that she was only looking out of herself."

"I *did* care." Tabitha began. "That was my problem. I cared about the little bastard, when I should've just sent him away with his mother."

"You've never cared about anyone but yourself!" Valerie hissed at her, as she fell into the chair behind her, sobbing with her head in her hands.

"And in all of these years? In all of these years, you never thought you should tell me?" I asked. "You never thought I could handle it?! Is that how little you think of me, Valerie?"

"No!" She said, desperately. "I wanted to tell you. I should've told you. I didn't know how. I'm so sorry Jackson. You have to believe me."

"I don't." I said. "I can't deal with this."

I pushed past Tabitha and made my way out of the living room, into the foyer. "You'll always be my son!" Tabitha shouted after me.

I turned to look at her, one last time.

"You can't escape that! I may not be in your blood, but I'm in your mind. And you'll never be rid of that,

Jackson. You LOVE me, God DAMN it!" She shouted, her voice shaking. There were tears in her eyes.

This was the first time I had ever seen my mother cry. I turned, slowly, and made my way out of the house.

Before I knew it, I found myself sitting alone at a bar. I couldn't tell you the name of the bar, or how I had gotten there. But there I was. All around me sat a mixture of happy couples and lonely losers, like myself, crying about the shitty cards life had dealt us. In front of me sat an empty glass.

"Excuse me?" I said to the bartender. "Could I get another?"

After a moment, the bartender moved towards me, a fresh drink in his hand. He set the vodka tonic down in front of me. I could feel him staring at me without looking up from the bar. "Do you need something?" I asked.

"It's just..." He began. "I think you've..."

"Let me guess." I began, sarcastically. "You think I've had enough to drink?"

"Y-ye...Yeah," He stammered.

"Look" I slurred back at him. "I'm not driving. So why do you care how much I want to drink?"

"You've been here for hours." He said. "You can barely sit up. I don't think it's healthy..."

I cut him off. "Oh, now you're a doctor!" I laughed.

"Look..." He said. "I'm just trying to help."

"I don't need your help." I said, as I stood. I slapped down a wad of money that Valerie had left in my room the day before. I turned and began to make my way towards the bathroom in the back of the bar. I stumbled, nearly knocking over several barstools on my way.

"Sorry." I mumbled to the sad, scary looking man sitting on one of the stools. He grunted an obscenity at me as I continued towards the restroom. When I reached the back of the restaurant, I pushed open the grimy door to the men's bathroom, locking it behind me. I moved slowly towards the already open toilet. Grabbing onto the cold, metal handlebars mounted on the wall, I fell forward at the waist as I threw up hours worth of drinks I didn't even remember drinking.

I fell to the floor, pushing myself up against the cold, dirty door. I caught my reflection in the bright metal of the toilet paper dispenser. My eyes were bloodshot and sad, vomit drying around the edges of my mouth. I let out a small laugh.

Finally, I found the strength to stand up. I splashed a handful of cold water in my face, careful not to catch my reflection in the mirror. I turned, unlocking the door and making my way back into the bar. Almost immediately, I collided with a young woman, carrying several drinks to a nearby table.

I fell to the ground in what felt like slow motion, watching as the glass shattered around me. I lay there, on the ground, for a long moment, an unsettling mixture of nausea and embarrassment flooding over me before I even opened my eyes.

And there she stood, standing, and smiling, above me.

It was Jules. My favorite nurse.

CHAPTER FIVE: The City

I felt the softness of cotton sheets against my cheek as I turned, exhaling, onto my left side. My eyes fluttered open and, slowly, I took in my surroundings. The small, apartment around me was cluttered to say the least, yet in the way that made you feel at home. Paintings and tapestries covered nearly every inch of wall space. Thick, brightly patterned curtains covered the industrial-sized windows, which looked out over a New York street not unlike any other. The tables were covered with papers, decorated with red rings where a wine glance had clearly once sat.

Where was I?

"Hey sleepy head." Said a soothing, female voice.

I looked up, startled, as I saw Jules standing across from me in the apartment's small kitchen. In that moment, it all came back to me – the fight, the bar, the bathroom, and most importantly: Jules. "What am I doing here?" I asked, my voice groggy.

"Do you not remember anything?" She asked, moving towards me with a glass of water in her hand. She handed me the glass. As I brought it to my lips to take a sip, she turned once more and made her way back to the kitchen. As she moved, her shirt rose slightly from her waist, revealing a small tattoo of a rose on her lower back.

"I remember being at the bar." I began, lowering the glass from my mouth. "And I remember falling, and then you being there. But that's it."

"You were pretty fucked up, I can't lie." She said, laughing. Standing by the stove now, she very delicately flipped what appeared to be a pancake, before beginning once again. "It was pretty difficult getting you out of there."

"Oh no..." I started. "Did I make a scene?"

"It could've been much worse." She laughed. "But the real bitch was trying to get you into a cab."

"Well, I'm glad you managed. Who knows where I would've woken up otherwise."

"Is that something that happens to you often?" She asked, jokingly, though there was a hint of seriousness in her tone, her eyebrows furrowed together ever so slightly.
"Not often." I began. "But maybe more often than I'm proud of."

"Well, I guess this was your lucky night." She said, as she turned her back to me, fumbling through the refrigerator. "I guess so." I said. There was a long pause. Jules continued her work in the kitchen, as I sat in her bed, silently. My mind raced as the previous night began to piece itself together in my mind.

"Why'd you bring me here?"

"What do you mean?" She asked, still not looking in my direction.

"You barely know me."

"That's really how you view the world, huh?" She asked.

"What do you mean?" I replied, taken aback.

"I overheard you have the same conversation with your nephew in the hospital. Why is it so hard for you to believe that people may want to help you?" She asked.

"Nobody ever really has."

She didn't answer me right away. Instead, she scooped the pancakes onto a bright yellow plate, grabbed the glass of milk she had just poured, and moved to her small kitchen table, setting the plate and cup down slowly. "Here." She said. "Come eat."

I stood from her bed. A wave of nausea came over me as a slight ringing filled my ears. I moved towards the kitchen table, taking the seat nearest to the cold air conditioner unit blowing from a nearby window. I sat there, my eyes closed for a moment, enjoying the cool breeze.

Jules finished what she was doing in the kitchen and, eventually, made her way to the kitchen table, her own breakfast in hand. She sat down next to me, taking a small bite of her pancake, before speaking. "I call bullshit." She said. I looked at her, confused. "What?"

"You said nobody's ever cared about you." She said. "I call bullshit."

"And why's that?" I shot back, almost angrily.

"Well, I just told you." She said. "I saw, firsthand, that your nephew cared about you when he visited you in the hospital." She paused again.

"And I helped you last night. I could care. But your first instinct is to doubt everyone, clearly. So I don't believe that nobody's cared about you, I just think that you don't let people show it." I took a bite of my food as her words settled in. "That's an awfully big assumption to make about someone you hardly know." I said.

"I can only base my opinion on what I've seen." She replied.

"Yes, and you've only seen me on suicide watch, and piss drunk. Those aren't exactly the most appropriate moments to make conclusions about someone." I said.

"I think those are the perfect moments to do so." She said, smiling.

Her words took me by surprise. I set my fork down on the plate and stood from the table. I walked across the small loft, towards her bed. Grabbing my t-shirt from the ground, I pulled it over my head. When I opened my eyes, Jules was standing in front of me, looking at me with compassion and humor. "Did I offend you?" She asked.

"You did." I said, coldly. "You know, I appreciate what you did for me, but you don't know me, and you can't just say shit like that."

"I didn't mean to hurt your feelings." She replied. "I was just trying to help."

"But why?" I asked, nearly shouting.

She looked at me, intently, for a few seconds, before moving to the other side of the room. Next to the couch sat a small, wooden table. On top of it was a small picture frame, which I hadn't noticed until now. Grabbing the picture, she turned and walked towards me once more. She handed me the frame, and in it was a photo of a young, teenaged boy. "Who is this?" I asked.

"That's my brother." She replied, her voice unsteady. "He killed himself last year."

I didn't know what to say.

I walked past Jules, slowly, towards the end table. I placed the picture back in its place and turned around. Looking at Jules, I could see the tears clouding her eyes. "Jules." I began. "I'm sorry. I didn't know."

"It's okay." She said, wiping her eyes. "I didn't tell you that to make you feel guilty." She paused. "He was quiet. Reserved, didn't let people in, but we were always close. I knew he was unhappy. He had demons - I knew that. I just didn't know how bad it was. We had a good childhood. Our parents loved us and they did the best that they could, but Jamie, he *always* had demons. I couldn't understand them, but I knew that, to him, they were the most real things in the world. He never could believe in himself the way I did. He always thought he was alone."

"I understand that feeling." I said, a lump rising in my throat.

"You're right, I don't know you." She began. "That's true. But I see your pain. Maybe it's because I've seen it before, maybe you just wear it on your sleeve. But I recognize it."

"I appreciate that. I really do." I said. "But you don't need to help me. You can't."

"How do you know?" She replied. "That's what I've never understood. I understand that depression is real; I understand that I *can't* understand certain things. But what I don't get is why I can't help."

"I can't speak for your brother, Jules." I said. "I didn't have a good childhood. I didn't have loving parents. This feeling, this state of mind, that's all I've ever known. I know that's sad, but this is my normal. Maybe it was his, too - I don't know. This thing, this depression, it goes so far beyond environment. It's something inside. I'd love to get better, but I don't know how. I don't know how to let someone help. I don't know how to make that change. But I know how to feel like this. This feeling, as terrible as it is, it's my comfortable. Maybe that's how your brother felt too."

"You must think I'm insane." She said, once again wiping away tears from her eyes.

"I don't really like that particular word." I said, softly.

"I'm sorry." She said, earnestly. "I know it's a lot. I bring you here, say some crazy shit and then play the dead brother card. I know how that must come across."

"I can tell that you care. That's a rare quality." I paused. "But you're not going to "save me", if that's what you had in mind." I turned from her and began making my way towards the door. "It was the anniversary." She said. "When they brought you in, it was the anniversary of Jamie's death." She was crying. "I wasn't even supposed to work that day, but they needed someone to cover a shift, and I said yes. I don't know why I did. Then I met you, and you told me your story, and I thought it was just some sick joke being played on me by a god I'm pretty sure doesn't even exist. Then I ran into you last night and maybe we're just "supposed" to know each other."

"That's not how things work, Jules." I began.

"He was a fan of yours." She said. The words knocked the wind from my chest.

"What did you say?" I asked.

"Your movies, or at least that one." She said. "With the little boy that dies?"

"*Geauga Lake.*" I said, laughing.

"Yes!" She shouted. "He loved that movie when he was a kid."

"I was 12 years old, playing a kid with terminal cancer." I laughed. "What an odd movie for a child to love."

"I know!" She said, laughing. "I always told him that. But he was like that, always in touch with his emotions; in a way I couldn't even understand. He loved stuff like that, stories that meant something." I smiled, but didn't say anything back.

"I didn't recognize you." She said. "But I recognized the name, so I looked you up. What are the odds that you would show up at my hospital, on the anniversary of my brother's death?"

"I'm flattered, truly, but that was just a movie. I'm nothing to aspire to, nothing to admire. Yes, it's kind of weird that our paths crossed, but I don't believe in any of that fate stuff."

"I don't either." She said. "But there's no way this is a coincidence, Jackson. I don't talk about my brother with anyone, not even my closest friends. You're right, I can't save you, but maybe we can help each other."

"I don't know what to say."

"Do you still have my number?" She asked

"I do." I said.

"Okay." She said. "Just think about it, and call me if you want to talk."

I nodded, moving towards the door and opening it slowly. I turned around and looked at her once more, before speaking.

"Thank you, for last night." I said. And with that, I left, closing the door behind me.

I spent most of the cab ride home in an odd state of shock. The driver attempted to make small talk with me on several occasions, though I didn't hear a word he said.

I had never believed in fate, or anything like that. I didn't have much reason to. Yet, I was filled with an uneasy feeling.

Eventually, the cab pulled up in front of Valerie's house. I handed the driver the last of the money Valerie had given me, and swung open the door to the cab. The sun was beating down hard, beads of sweat forming almost instantly on my forehead. Several people were roaming the streets, including Valerie's next-door neighbor, who I had never met, but who loved to shoot me dirty looks. I smiled and waved at him softly. He turned, pretending not to see me.

I made my way through the gate, to the entryway of the house. Entering the foyer, I instantly heard the sound of voices from the nearby living room. I wanted, desperately, to avoid any conversation with my sister and, thus, immediately made my way to the steps. Unfortunately, she heard me come in. "Jackson?" She shouted. "Is that you?" I paused for a moment. "Yes."

"Come in here for a moment." A voice replied. But it wasn't Valerie's voice this time. It was Charles'. I exhaled deeply, before making my way to the living room. "Hello Jackson." Charles said, as I entered the room. "Hello." I replied, avoiding eye contact.

"Please, have a seat." He said. Reluctantly, I sat in the plush white chair next to the fireplace. "I was worried sick." Valerie said. I looked at her for the first time since entering the room. Her hair was disheveled, her makeup streaked. She was wearing the same clothes that I had last seen her in the night before.

"I'm fine." I said.

"I just think we need to talk about things, Jackson." She said. "I have so much I want to tell you."

"Yeah, I'm not really interested in talking to you right now." I snapped back.

"Then you can get the fuck out of our house!" Charles bellowed back at me.

I stared intently at the floor in front of me, refusing to make eye contact.

"Charles!" Valerie shouted, her voice shaking. "Please!" Nobody spoke for several seconds.

"You know, I don't appreciate this." Charles said. His voice was much calmer now, yet still threatening. I didn't reply. "Every time you show up here, there's some type of drama." He continued. "Now I've got my wife sitting here in tears, with an eight year old and a teenager upstairs that I've got to worry about. I can't have their lives disrupted by your bullshit."

"You think I don't know that?" I asked, coldly. "I didn't come here to cause any problems."

"Yet they seem to follow you wherever you go." He replied.

"Charles, the last time I was here you were quite thrilled. Or are you forgetting that?" I replied, my jaw clenched.

"You showed up, unable to take care of yourself, as usual, and we made an arrangement that was beneficial for both of us. You didn't do me any favors."

"Please!" Valerie said, through tears. "That's enough! Both of you!"

"You know, it's funny, Valerie." I said. "You have a lot to say when I'm in your house, but yet you were dead silent for the past 10 years – about information that could've made things a hell of a lot easier for me."

"That's not fair." She said.

"Not fair?" I shouted back at her, standing from the chair. "What isn't fair was you lying to me for a goddamn DECADE. You were supposed to be the only person who had my back, yet you're just as selfish as our –excuse me, your—mother."

"That's not true."

"You didn't tell me the truth because, what – you were jealous? Livid at the idea that I could get away from that woman and have a real family?"

She stood from her chair, angrily.

"That is not true!" She shouted. "I have done everything in my power to help you! I made a mistake and I am sorry for that, but I have been damn good to you,

Jackson! You show up here, I give you a place to stay. Just like we helped you then."

"Those things are wonderful, Val, certainly ups your charity points, but it doesn't change the fact that you thought so little of me for all these years. That you never had the courtesy to tell me the truth about my own life."

"Have you ever considered that maybe she doesn't think much of you at all?" Charles began. "Because you don't provide anything for anyone to think much of?"

Before I could stop it, there were tears in my eyes. Eventually, he spoke again.

"I think I've always treated you like a brother, Jackson." He said. "But this cannot continue. I'm sorry for what you're going through, but you can't come in here and wreak havoc. You disappear, you upset my wife, and my son finds you half dead in your room. Your problems cannot be everyone's problems, Jackson." He left the room before I could reply. Eventually, Valerie moved towards me once more. She leaned in, kissing me on the forehead. "Your problems are my problems, Jackson." She said, softly. "Whether you believe it or not, I'm sorry." She turned and began to leave the room.

"I love you Val."

"I love you, too." She said.

I sat in the same spot for what felt like hours, my mind racing faster than usual. It took all of my willpower to fight the urge to pour myself a drink. Eventually, I heard someone enter the foyer. I stood from my chair, making my way into the front hall.

"Austin." I said.

"Hey!" He said.

"Let's go somewhere."

"Okay." He replied. "Where are we going?"

"I'll explain when we get there."

After two trains and over ten blocks walked, we finally reached a small alley, tucked in a corner of the city I had never shared with anyone before. "What is this place?" We made our way down the dimly lit steps into the alley, and through a creaky wooden door with a "Welcome to Madam Nicoletta's Book Shop" sign on the front. I watched as Austin's eyes grew, taking in the cozy room and it's thick, incense laden scent.

"This is my place." I replied.

"What do you mean?" He asked, confused.

"When I was younger, I used to come here." I answered, moving across the small room, to a pair of sagging, pink velvet chairs. "I don't even remember how I found it, but it's just the most peaceful place. There are no windows, either. It's the only place in city where you can't hear or see a million different things."

He listened for a moment.

"That's so weird." He said.

"I can't explain it, but it's like it's this weird little piece of solidarity in the middle of this ridiculous city."

"Do you bring people here often?" He asked.

"You're the first." I said.

"Why me?"

"This is where I came the first time." I paused. "The first time that I wanted to kill myself. Or, I should say, the first time I was actually going to try. I got scared, though, and somehow ended up here."

He didn't reply right away. I could tell he was fighting back tears.

"I still don't understand why you'd bring me here." He said, his voice trembling, filled with a defensive sadness.

"When I got here, I was ready to go, but I came here, and I sat right here and read, for hours and hours. There's so much beauty in these books, in all art. I thought, what if there's more? What if there's more like this in the world out there for me? What if I die now and I never get to experience that? I want to share that with you, because I believe there is beauty out there, for you. And if you ever lose sight of that, I want you to be able to come here, to remember."

He began crying. "So you just got here and decided not to do it?" He asked.

"I got here and I thought about what else is out there. I made a deal with myself, that I would try to find a reason to live."

"So what was your reason?" He asked, sincerely. "What changed?"

"A few nights later, when I got home, I found a letter that someone had slid underneath my door." I said. "I found something out that changed just about everything."

"What was it?" He asked.

"That I had a daughter."

CHAPTER SIX: Another World

Austin looked at me for a long moment before opening his mouth to speak.
"You have a what?" He asked, incredulously. "A daughter." I said.

"I don't understand." He replied, confusedly. "I've never heard anything about you having a daughter before."

"Most people don't know." I replied.

"But you're telling me?"

"I am."

"Why?"

"She's been on my mind lately."

"What happened? Where is she?"

"I suppose I should start from the beginning." I said, with a chuckle.

"I've pretty much been on my own since I was fifteen." I said. "When I wasn't a cute kid anymore, and the work stop coming, my mother didn't waste much time before heading back to Maine. She left me out there, I suppose with the hopes that I could still make her some money from time to time."

"You were all on your own?" He asked.

"Pretty much." I replied.

"I can't even imagine." He started. "I'm 17 and I could never."

"That's the problem." I said. "I was a child, but nobody was treating me like one."

"So what did you do out there?" He asked.

"All the wrong things." I replied. "It didn't take long at all before I was introduced to partying and drugs and all kinds of dangerous shit that I shouldn't have been involved in."

"Dangerous how?" He asked.

"Drugs, mostly." I began. "But we took it to a whole different level. The people I was hanging around with didn't just use drugs - they used people. They stole and they used and they manipulated. They were always looking for a come up, but at the time, I didn't see any of that. I was young, and stupid, and just looking for somewhere to fit in."

"So what happened?"

"I turned 18, and things were really bad by then. I was blowing through my money, I had cut pretty much everyone else out of my life. I was in a dark place, and having all of that money was the last thing I needed. I bought a house and I was paying for everything. Drugs, food, clothes, vacations. I thought that's what friendship was. Isn't that sad?"

He didn't reply.

"Anyway, as you might imagine, the money didn't last forever. And once it was gone, so were they."

"That's fucked up." He said.

"It was." I replied. "I told them I was broke, and within a week they were all gone. I came home one day and their things were just gone from the house. There was no note, no forwarding address, no phone number. They were done with me, just like that."

"So what did you do?" He asked.

"Well, I knew I couldn't stay in L.A .anymore." I started, clearing my throat and sighing. "So I called my mother. I told her I was in trouble. She didn't care much, but she did send me some money. She didn't ask me to come home, but she sent me a check. So I got on a plane to New York, and I told myself I was going to start over. It didn't take long for me to fuck that up, though."

"That's awful." He said.

"It wasn't great." I began. "I was lucky enough to have some friends around the city that would let me spend a night here and there on their couch, but eventually I burned those bridges, too. I convinced my mother to send me a little more money and I rented a shitty studio apartment. But I was so embarrassed by the fact that I even needed her money. I wasn't even getting out of bed for days at a time. By then, I knew I didn't want to do it anymore."

"Do what?" He asked.

"Live." I replied.

"Oh." He said.

"I was so embarrassed, and lonely, and sad." I said. "One day, I forced myself to get out of bed and go somewhere, anywhere. Somehow I wound up here, and for whatever reason, I felt like everything might be okay."

"So what happened next?" He asked. "When did you get the letter?"

"Three or four nights later." I said. "I had a friend in LA named Adam. He was the first one from that group that I met, at an audition. He introduced me to the rest of that group. We were all around the same age, except for Carlotta, Adam's older sister. She was about ten years older than us, and she was beautiful, the type of beautiful that could just captivate you, without saying a word. She'd just gotten out of some shitty relationship and she ended up living with us. I thought she was the love of my life."

"I'm assuming it didn't end well?" Austin asked.

"When the money dried up, she was the first to disappear."

"I'm sorry." He said.

"It's okay, it was a long time ago." I assured him. "When I got back to my apartment that day, I found the letter from her, telling me she was pregnant. I didn't believe it, honestly. I assumed it was just her trying to see if there was any last drop of money she could squeeze out of me. But I knew I would never forgive myself if I didn't find out for sure."

"So what did you do?" He asked.

"I asked your mother for the money to go back to LA." I paused, looking at him.
"When I got there, I tracked Carlotta down and told her I was moving in with her. I was worried she was using."

"And was she?" He asked.

"Thankfully, no." I replied. "So we waited until a paternity test could be done and as it turned out, she wasn't lying."

"Wow." Austin said, quietly. "So what did you do? Give her up for adoption?"

"Carlotta wanted to." I began. "She was in no position to be raising a child, and neither was I. She wanted to give the baby up for adoption, but I couldn't stand the thought of it. I begged her to let me keep her. Eventually she agreed, and after our daughter was born, I took her and left for New York. I never saw Carlotta again."

"But how did you take care of her?"

"It wasn't easy." I started. "I was too embarrassed to even call Valerie, because I knew she would worry and overextend herself trying to help me. So I called my mother. She didn't really want anything to do with me, or my daughter, but she agreed to support us, at least temporarily. So she set me up a bank account and a better apartment, and I was grateful for that, even if it was the least she could've done. Everything was okay, for a minute."

"What do you mean?" He asked.

"I loved that girl more than anything in the world." I began; blinking back the hot tears I could feel welling up in my eyes. "All I wanted was to be a good father, but I was a kid. I had no idea what I was doing. I started using again, blowing through all of the money. It was bad."

"So you gave her up for adoption?" He asked.

"I sent her to live with a wonderful family, who I knew could take better care of her than I'd ever be able to."

"I can't imagine how hard that must've been." Austin said, placing his hand on my shoulder. "I'm sorry."

"It was the hardest thing I ever had to do." I said. "But it was the right thing to do."

Neither of us spoke for a long moment.

"Do you know where she's at now? Have you ever spoken to her?"

"I know she's okay, but she doesn't know about me. That was the agreement."

"Oh." He replied.

"Yeah." I replied, wiping my face. "I didn't come here to upset you. I just wanted to show you this place, and tell you what it's done for me. I hope it can do the same for you."

"Thank you, Uncle Jackson." He said, blinking back the tears in his own eyes. "I've never really had someone trust me like that before."

"You've always got a friend in me, kid" I said. "Now, let's get out of here."

We walked towards the subway terminal, neither of us speaking much. My mind raced a mile a minute, thinking of our conversation, of that place, of my daughter. Finally, after nearly 45 minutes, we reached the house. Austin removed his key ring from his pocket, unlocking both the gate and the front door, letting us into the house. After closing the door behind us, he turned to face me once more. Reaching his arms out, we embraced in a long hug.

"Thank you." He said. "Goodnight."

With that, he made his way up the stairs. After several seconds, I heard his bedroom door close behind him. I decided to go into the kitchen for an evening snack and to my surprise, I found Valerie perched at the granite island, wine glass in hand.

"Hey Val." I said, softly.

She looked up, surprised. Clearly, she hadn't heard me enter the room. She was dressed in silk pajamas, her face makeup free, hair pulled back in a sloppy ponytail. I had rarely, if ever, seen her like this before.

"Oh." She said. "You're home."

"Yeah, I just got here." I replied.

"Did you go somewhere with Austin?" She asked.

"Yeah, we just went for a little walk. We were talking, mostly."

"That's nice." She said, genuinely. "I'm glad you two are spending time together."

"Really?" I asked, surprised.

"You're his uncle." She said. "Austin needs someone."

"What about his father?" I asked, only half serious.

"Charles is hardly around, and when have you ever known him to talk about his own feelings, let alone ask someone about theirs?" She said, pausing to take a sip from her wine glass. "Austin is going through something. I don't know what, but he is. He's always been an emotional kid, but he won't talk to me. He won't go to therapy. I'm his mother, I know something is wrong, and I just want to help him. But I don't know how. If he's opening up to you, that's great. Maybe you can."

"I'm probably the last person who should be helping anyone with their life." I replied.

"You're a good person, Jackson, and maybe that's all Austin needs. Someone to listen to him, to help him avoid the mistakes our mother never bothered to shield us from." With that, she took one large, final sip, draining her wine glass.

For several moments, neither of us spoke. I fumbled through the fridge, looking for something that appeared even slightly appetizing, while Valerie made her way across the kitchen to pour another glass of wine. Eventually, she spoke once more.

"I really thought I was protecting you." She said, softly.

"What?" I asked, caught off guard.

"By not telling you."

"Val" I started. "We don't have to do this."

"No." She said, cutting me off. "We do. You deserve answers."

I moved across the kitchen, sitting on the tall barstool where Valerie had sat just moments beforehand.

"When I found the letter, I was livid." She began. "I must've read it a hundred times before I really understood it. I was so mad. I didn't understand. I mean I could almost wrap my head around the idea that you were adopted and that she never told you that. What I didn't understand was how she could take you in, agree to raise you as her own, and treat you so terribly. Yes, she treated me terribly, too, but I was a burden she didn't ask for. She CHOSE to take you in. She CHOSE to treat you that way. That's what I didn't understand."

"What did she say when you confronted her?" I asked.

"She refused to give me any details. She told me it was none of my business, but that didn't stop her from her usual manipulation." Valerie replied.

"What do you mean?" I asked.

"She got in my head, deliberately." She started. "She knew you were hanging out with all the wrong people out there in LA, but she also knew you had gotten clean around that time."

"Yeah, for about a minute." I said, interrupting her. "I just told her I was clean so she wouldn't take my money away. I knew she didn't care enough to actually come and check."

"Yeah well she didn't tell me that. She told me you were clean. She convinced me that if I told you the truth, that it would hurt you, that you'd start using again. I was stupid to believe her, but I did. I just didn't want to hurt you. I wanted to protect you, but I hurt you. And I'm sorry."

"It's okay, Val." I said.

"It's not!" She said, tears welling up in her eyes. "I owed you more than that. All these years have passed, and I should have told you. But I was scared, I was selfish."

"Nobody's perfect." I replied. "Besides, I doubt it would've made much difference. By the time you found out, I was pretty fucked up already. My bed was made. There's nothing you could've done. I shouldn't have lashed out at you the way I did."

"You had every right to." She replied.

"Not really." I said. "Not considering I did the same thing to my own daughter."

"Jackson." Valerie began. "That's not fair. It's not the same."

"What's different about it, Val?" I replied, my voice cracking. "I gave my daughter up and demanded she never know about me. I like to say I was protecting her, but I was just being a coward. As usual."

"That isn't true, Jackson. You did what you felt was best for your daughter. You know that our mother's motivations were not the same. You are nothing like her, Jackson."

I didn't reply. Instead, I stared intently at the food in front of me, which I had failed to take even one bite of. My mind was racing, my heart pounding as tears filled my eyes. After a moment, Valerie made her way towards me, placing her cool hand on mine as she reached the island where I was seated.

"She's sick, Jackson."

I looked up at her, confused.

"What?" I asked.

"Mom." Valerie started. "She's sick."

"Sick with what?"

"I don't know, but I got a voicemail from a doctor's office. They said something about her staying here after she begins treatment. I guess she listed me as her emergency contact.. I called back, but the office was closed."

"Why didn't she say anything?" I asked, half to myself.

"Who knows."

"So you think it's serious?" I asked.

"I don't know, but the message didn't sound great." She replied.

Neither of us spoke for a moment. Val wrapped her arm around my shoulder, resting her head on mine. We stayed like this for several seconds. Eventually, I stood from the island, facing my sister once more.

That's when I noticed it - a fresh new bruise on the left side of her neck.

My heart started pounding once more, my mind going blurry for a moment. Before I could stop myself, I said it.

"Is Charles hitting you?"

A look of terror spread across her face. Instantly, her eyes filled with tears.

"Why would you ask me that?" She said, turning away from me.

"I've seen the bruises, the cuts and scrapes. I tried to keep my mouth shut, but I can't. Our mother is one of the most miserable, unhappy people I've ever met, and I've always thought that maybe part of that was because she was trapped in such a shitty marriage for so long. That misery is all she knows, and I won't let that happen to you." I said, firmly. "Valerie, if he's hitting you, you have to tell me."

"Don't be ridiculous." She said, still not facing me.

"Valerie!" I said, loudly, my voice shaking.

After several seconds, she turned to look at me once more. Her face was soaked with tears. Her hand trembled as she refilled her wine glass once more.

"It wasn't always like this." She said, quietly.

I didn't say a word. Eventually, she began again.

"We were happy, always. He never, ever laid a hand on me. I would've never stayed with a man that did that, let alone had kids with him."

"So this started after the kids?" I asked.

"Yes." She replied, shaking slightly. "A few years ago, things got bad. He made some bad investments, really bad. His businesses were failing and his business partner sold him down the river. It was terrible for him. It broke him, it really did."

"Please don't defend him, Valerie." I said.

"I'm not!" She began. "But something changed in him then. I don't know what it was, but something broke. Something changed, in his eyes even. The man I fell in love with wasn't there. Then one day they came, and they took one of the cars, and he was so mad, and so upset, and that was the first time he hit me. I didn't know what to do. I felt like my whole world was collapsing around me, Jackson. This was a man I loved, who I'd known most of my life, who I had children with. I watched him turn into a monster, right in front of my own eyes."

"Why didn't you leave?" I asked, softly.

"I wanted to believe it was a one time thing, but the worse things got, the more it started to happen. Then he got the businesses together, somehow. He got us back on our feet, and I thought things would change, but they only got worse. He never went back to being the man I loved. He only got more and more violent. I wanted to leave, but I knew he'd leave me with nothing. I knew he'd take my kids from me, Jackson. My lawyer told me to snoop, to find something, anything that I could use against him. I had a feeling that not everything he'd been doing was legitimate, and I thought if I could find proof, that it could be my way out."

"So what happened?"

"I found out that his illegal dealings went even farther back than I was aware of."

"How far back?" I asked.

"All the way back." She paused, wiping her eyes. "Everything, from the time we first got married. It was all a scam., and I was so stupid. I can admit that. When we first got married I was young and dumb and so eager to get away from our mother, and I signed anything and everything he put in front of me. I never read anything. I trusted him, like an idiot."

"Valerie..."

"I took a bunch of documents to my lawyer and he basically told me that Charles had been playing me all along. If he was going down, I was going down harder. I was trapped. I AM trapped. Every day I have to pray that he won't hit my children. Every day I have to pray that he won't get caught, that he won't take me down with him."

"Jesus Christ." I said, incredulously. "But can't you still leave? He's not going to turn himself in just to take you down with him. You said you'd go down harder than he will, but that doesn't mean he won't still go down, right? He'll still get in trouble with the law, right? He's not going to risk that."

"He's a powerful man, Jackson." Valerie said. "He'll take my kids. I know he will. He knows people, he has connections that I don't have. He'll take my kids. He'll do something, anything. He'll get rid of me somehow. He's not a good man."

I didn't know how to reply. I stood from my chair and moved towards her, wrapping my arms tightly around her.

"I'm going to bed." She whispered, finally. "Please, don't say anything about this, Jackson. We can talk more, but please, don't do anything rash. I'm begging you, for my sake, for the kids. I don't know what he's capable of, Jackson, and I don't want to find out."

"Okay, Val." I said. "I love you."

"I love you, too." She said, leaving the room.

A moment later, I made my way to the bathroom located off the foyer. Opening the medicine cabinet, I fumbled through the bottles until I found one labeled "Hydrocodone". Taking it in my hand, I shut the medicine cabinet and made my way to the living room. I grabbed the decanter of vodka from the sidebar and raised it to my lips, taking a large swig. After a moment, I opened the bottle of pills in my hand and placed several in my mouth, washing them down with a large swig of vodka. Taking the vodka with me, I made my way to the couch, where I continued to drink until I fell asleep.

At some point I heard Charles come into the house, loudly. My mind was foggy and I struggled to stay awake. I heard as he made his way to the den. The next thing I could remember was Valerie begging him to keep his voice down. He shouted at her, loudly, calling her several cruel names. I heard the sound of his hand striking her.

I tried with everything I had to stand, to defend my sister, to get him away from her, but I couldn't move. Slowly, I drifted back to sleep.

When I awoke again, I was laying on the cold marble ground of the foyer. I stayed there for several seconds, letting the cold of the tile against my cheek bring me back to consciousness. Finally, I found the strength to stand.

What had happened?

I turned to make my way towards the stairs, but as I did so, I noticed the doors to Charles' den were left wide open. This was unusual, as he always kept the den closed and locked. Curious, I began to move, slowly, towards the open doors.

As I neared the den, my eyes widened as they took in the sight in front of them. The den was torn to shreds. Papers were scattered across the desk and floor, pictures lay broken on the ground. The curtains hung crooked from their frame around the window.

Slowly, I looked down at the ground in front of me. There he was, face down on the room's hardwood floor. A pool of blood surrounded his head.

There was Charles.

Dead.

CHAPTER SEVEN: One Life to Live

I stood there, staring at Charles' lifeless body on the ground in front of me. Time stood still. The room began to spin around me, my breaths short and sharp.

It wasn't long before I heard footsteps moving towards me. Turning around, I saw Valerie standing at the foot of the staircase, a look of horror etched across her pale face. Slowly, she began to move towards me, making her way past me, through the doorway and towards Charles. She stood, silently, for several seconds. Using her left arm, she reached towards the large wooden desk, bracing herself as she closed her eyes, breathing in slowly and deeply. "What happened?" She asked, her voice a thin whisper.

"I don't know."

She opened her eyes. "Is he dead?" She asked, coldly.

"I think so."

"Check." She said. "Please."

I moved towards Charles' body. Stepping over the growing pool of blood, I knelt down next to him and pressed my fingers to his neck. I waited like this for several long seconds before looking at my sister once more. I nodded.

She stared in my direction, silently. Her gaze was locked directly with mine, yet she wasn't looking at me. Her eyes were glassy and distant. She let out a long, quaking breath as she slid to the floor, covering her face with her hands. Standing quickly, I moved towards my sister, unsure of what to say. I knelt down next to her, wrapping my arms around her shoulders.

"What do we do?" She said, softly, looking up at me. Her words didn't register with me. The alcohol on her breath, however, did.

"Valerie" I said. "Have you been drinking?"

"What?" She said, confused. "What the fuck kind of question is that?"

"It's just - I smell it on your breath, is all." I replied.

"Jackson, what are you talking about? What does that have to do with anything? My husband is dead and you're asking me if I've been drinking? You saw me drinking earlier, when you came home! I was drinking then!"

"That was hours ago, Val." I began. "You smell like you just had a drink."

She pushed my arms off of her shoulders aggressively and stood up, stumbling slightly.

"And just what are you insinuating?" She said, angrily, as she turned to look at me once more.

"I'm not insinuating anything, Val!" I replied. "I overheard you and Charles arguing..."

"And what?" She hissed, cutting me off. "You think I got sloshed and killed my husband?"

"Of course not." I replied. "I'm sorry."

"How do I know you didn't do it?" She asked, defensively. "How do I know you didn't get up from your drunken stupor and kill him yourself?"

"I shouldn't have said anything." I began. "I just want to protect you."

"And how far are you willing to go to do that?" She replied.

"I didn't kill Charles."

"Neither did I."

That was a lie. Or rather, it might've been. The truth was, I couldn't remember. I wasn't convinced that I hadn't. But then, I wasn't convinced that she hadn't, either.

"Okay, then." I said, exhaling slowly. "Then I guess we call the police."

"We can't do that!" She replied, shouting quietly. Before I could answer her, the sound of steps came once more from the stairwell. There was Austin, standing at the foot of the stairs, his eyes wide with confusion and terror.

"What..." He began.

"Austin!" Valerie shouted, cutting him off and rushing to his side. "Austin, please. Go back upstairs! Go!"

"Mom…" He started.

"Austin!" She yelled, cutting him off once more. "Please. Go upstairs. Sit in your sister's room. You make sure she doesn't come down here. Please, Austin. Go. You shouldn't be here. You have to go upstairs, please!"

Reluctantly, Austin turned and began making his way back up the stairs. When he reached the top, he turned towards us once more. For a long moment, he stared at his father's body, blank faced. Eventually, he turned and made his way down the hallway, closing his sister's bedroom door softly behind him.

"What do you mean, we can't call the police?" I whispered, frantically. "There's a dead man in your den. What are we supposed to do?"

"Jackson, I didn't kill him…" She said, her hand wiping away the fresh tears in her eyes. Her first tears since coming down those stairs. "You already told me that…" I began.

"But they'll think I did!" She replied, yelling. "The wife is always the first suspect."

"But there's no proof." I said.

"They'll see the bruises and scratches. They'll find out that I was seeing a divorce lawyer. They'll find out that I was digging things up on him. I'll practically be handing them my motive!"

"If you didn't do it, they won't be able to convict you, Valerie. They'll find the real killer." I replied.

"Oh, don't be naïve, Jackson!" She spat. "My husband is dead in my house, murdered, and I have all the motive in the world. I don't have an alibi! They're not even going to *look* outside of this house for the killer. They won't have to. They'll have a million signs pointing in my direction."

"So, I'll give you an alibi." I replied. She didn't say anything. "I'll tell them that we were together."

"That's not exactly a convincing alibi, Jackson." She replied. "You're my brother, they'll think you're lying for me."

"We'll tell them we were upstairs." I began. "Watching a movie. The theater room is sound proof - you can't hear anything from in there. It would make sense that we might not have heard a struggle. And..." I said, pausing to think. "We were coming down to get more wine before watching another movie. That's when we found him."

She hesitated for several seconds. "I don't know..." She said, slowly. "What if they see right through it?"

"It's a lot less suspicious than us telling them we were both blackout drunk and slept through a goddamn murder." I said.

"But that's the truth!" She replied, exasperated. So she *was* drinking. More than the two glasses of wine I'd seen.

"Yeah, well sometimes the truth gets you fucked." I replied, ignoring her slip up.

"But is it smart to lie to the police?" She asked.

"A minute ago you didn't even want to call them!"

"Okay." She said, quietly.

"Okay." I replied. "I'm going to take a couple of the used wine glasses up to the movie room and leave them there. I'll pop a DVD in the projector, too. Clueless. That was always our favorite. We can answer questions about that movie, if it comes to that."

"Why are you doing all that?" She asked.

"If we tell them we were in the theater room while he was being attacked, they're obviously going to snoop around up there. We need to make it look like we were actually in there."

"Oh, right." She replied, distantly.

After my staging of the theater room, I returned downstairs and instructed Valerie to phone the police. She did so, putting on her most frantic voice as she told the 911 operator that her husband had been murdered.

The police arrived within moments of the call, and immediately turned the entire first floor of the house into a full-on crime scene. For hours, each of us answered the officers' hundreds of questions.

We gave our official statements, both providing similar variations of our planned story. Whether they bought our story or not was relatively unclear, and that didn't make the situation any less intimidating. Finally, just as the sun began to rise outside the foyer's picturesque window, I was informed that my role was complete, at least for the time being.

"Mr. Arrington…" Began the stoic, somewhat intimidating Detective Lewis. "We don't have any further questions for you at this moment."

"So can I go check on my children now?" Valerie asked, desperately.

"I'm afraid not." Replied Detective Lewis. "We have a few more question for you."

"It's okay, Val." I said. "I'll go check on them."

"That reminds me…" Detective Lewis started. "I'm going to need to question them, as well."

Fuck. And there it was. The one thing we hadn't thought of.

Just then, I noticed him. At the top of the stairs was Austin, clearly listening to the conversation at hand. We made eye contact, as a look of terror spread over my face. He nodded at me, ever so slightly.

"Officer…" I began.

"Detective." He corrected me.

"I'm sorry." I replied. "Detective. The kids were fast asleep. Valerie had just checked on them right before we came downstairs. They couldn't have heard a thing."

"It looks like there was a pretty big struggle here." Detective Lewis said, his eyes squinting suspiciously as he pondered the scenario aloud. "Seems like it'd be pretty hard to sleep through." I didn't know how to reply. My mouth went dry. And then he spoke.

"I take sleeping pills, detective." Austin said, making his way down the steps. "I don't sleep well at all, so I stock up on those over the counter sleep meds. They knock me out like you wouldn't believe. I could sleep through a tornado. You can go and check in my bathroom, I have like three boxes in the medicine cabinet."

"So you had no knowledge of your father's murder until when, exactly?" Detective Lewis asked him, his expression softening.

"I woke up to use the restroom and I heard my mother and uncle speaking down here. I realized how late it was and I knew something was wrong. I came to the top of the stairs and called down to them. My mother rushed over and told me to stay in my room, but I saw..." He paused, wiping his eyes. "I saw my father laying there. My mother didn't want me to see him like that. She asked me to go sit with my sister."

Had Valerie mentioned to Detective Lewis anything about speaking to Austin during all of this? Had I? If not, did Austin's lie put a hole in our story? I couldn't remember, and I began to fear that our plan was falling apart.

Detective Lewis moved closer to Austin. He placed her arm on his shoulder.

"I'm sorry for your loss, son." He began. "And I'm sorry you had to find out the way you did."

So he believed us. Or is that just what he wanted us to think?

"I may still need to ask you a few questions, young man. And I will need to speak to your daughter, Mrs. Sinclair."

"Please!" Valerie began, tears forming in her eyes. "She is an eight year old child. She doesn't even know that her father is dead. Do you think if she did, she'd be upstairs sleeping in her bed? She's a child for Christ's sake. Please, leave her out of this."

Detective Lewis pondered this for a moment, before speaking. "I can't make any guarantees that we won't need to speak to her down the line."

"Thank you." Valerie said, sincerely.

"Now, Mrs. Sinclair, I still have a few questions for you."

"I'll go check on Madeleine while you do that." I said. "Austin, why don't you come with me?" The two of us climbed the stairs, as Detective Lewis continued to question Valerie.

We made our way down the hall, towards Madeleine's room. Slowly, quietly, I cracked the door and peered inside. There she was, sleeping like a baby. As if nothing had happened. I opened the door fully, making my way inside. Austin stayed behind, looming quietly in the doorway.

I made my way over to her bed. Reaching down, I brushed the hair from in front of her face and looked at her for several seconds. I had hardly interacted with her since I had moved in. I was afraid to. I was afraid to damage her. Now, with Charles gone, I knew I'd have to step up. For the first time in my life, I was going to have to have to be there for my family.

I leaned down and kissed her softly on the forehead. As I turned towards the door, I realized Austin was no longer standing there. I moved quietly across the room, shutting the door softly behind me. Quickly, I made my way to Austin's room, entering without knocking. He looked at me, intently, without saying a word.

"Are you okay?" I blurted out, clumsily, unsure of what else to say.

"Yeah. " He replied.

"You know, it's okay not to be." I started.

"He wasn't a good man." He said, sternly, cutting me off.

"Austin..." I started.

"He wasn't." He began. "Yet I idolized him. I always wanted him to approve of me. I always thought maybe then things would be easier, if I was like him. He just made me so mad."

"What do you mean?" I asked.

"He had this beautiful life and a family and an amazing wife and he took all of that for granted. I've never felt normal. I've never felt like I belonged in this family. I never felt like I could impress him, like I could be his equal. I knew he was a bad man, I knew he hit my mom, but I still held him on this pedestal. I just, I guess I just wanted him to be proud of me, even though his opinion shouldn't have meant anything to me."

"That's normal, Austin." I replied.

"Is it?" He asked. "Is it normal to strive for the approval of someone you know is a monster?"

"When that person is your parent, yes. I think it is." I said.

"I could see the type of person he was. I knew I didn't want to be like him. I knew he was an asshole, but he just made me feel so bad about myself. I started to believe that maybe I was a freak. That maybe I was supposed to be like him. I have this wonderful mother, yet that was never enough for me. I was always striving for his approval. What's wrong with me?"

"There's nothing wrong with you, Austin. He was not a good man, but he was your father. He was the only one you had. You loved him, and I'm sure he loved you, in his own way. The way he treated you was wrong. He didn't act like a father is supposed to, and you didn't know that. You didn't know there was anything better out there -that HE was supposed to be better."

"He treated me like shit, and that's one thing, but he treated my mother terribly, and I let it happen. What kind of person does that make me?"

"It makes you an innocent child in all of this." I began, sitting next to him on the edge of his bed. "You were put in a terrible, awful situation, one that no child should be in. You had a man who was supposed to love you unconditionally, who was supposed to be your role model, and he didn't act that way. I understand, more than anyone, the impact that has on a person. But it's not your fault, nothing was your fault."

"Do you feel that way?" He asked, looking at me. "Do you feel that way about your mom?"

I paused for a moment.

"I did." I began. "For a very long time, I did. My father was never around, ever, and I made my peace with that. I suppose mother wasn't around all that much either, as I got older, but she was the constant parent in my life, and she was not very nice. I did strive for her approval. I never understood why she treated me the way she did. Even today I don't really, fully understand it. Yet even though I knew she was wrong, even though I knew that she was not a good mother, I still just wanted her to love me, because that's what we're supposed to get from our parents. Love. Acceptance. Understanding. And when we don't get those things, it can really fuck us up. That doesn't mean there's anything wrong with us."

"So you don't feel like that anymore?" He asked. "You don't still want her approval?"

"I guess, one day, I just realized that I don't need it." I said. "I believe my mother loves me, in her own twisted way. I don't need anything else from her. We don't need the approval of people like that. They're the ones who treat us poorly, who do these terrible things. We didn't deserve to be treated that way. We didn't do anything wrong. Why would we want their approval? In fact, I think, if we did have it, it would say something *negative* about us, in a way." He sat silently for several seconds.

"Yeah." He said. "I guess you're right."

I patted him on the shoulder, before standing to leave. As I reached the door, he spoke once more.

"Thank you." He said.

"Of course." I replied.

"No really, thank you." He said. "Having you here has been great."

I moved towards him, sitting on the bed once more.

"Austin..." I began. "I've been where you are. Maybe not the exact circumstance, but that pain you're feeling, I've felt it. And, when I did, there wasn't really anybody around to help me through it. Your mother did the best that she could, but by the time things were really bad for me, she was grown and on her own, with her own life. I was alone a lot, and I always wished there had been someone there to say these things to me. I guess I just say to you the things that I wish someone had said to me."

"Thank you." He replied.

"You're welcome." I said, getting up to leave. Once more, however, he stopped me in my tracks.

"I know you lied." He said.

I turned to face him.

"I know you and my mom were lying to the police, about something, about the way things happened tonight. That's why I lied, too, and I'll lie for you again, if I have to. I'll do whatever I have to do to protect you and my mother."

My heart sank. One more burden placed on this kid. One more adult situation he should never have had to deal with. "We can talk about this some other time." I said. "Just know that your mother and I both love you very much, and we only want what's best for you."

The next few days flew by in what felt like the world's longest nightmare. The police came in and out of the house non-stop, examining and re-examining the same things over and over, asking the same questions hundreds of times. Madeleine took the news of her father's passing hard, and spent most nights crying out for him in her sleep. She only knew the good in her father, what little of it there had been.

I could see how hard this was for Valerie, and I only wished I knew of a better way to help. After nearly a week, things showed no sign of slowing down, and the question of a funeral had come up more than once. Neither Valerie nor I were terribly interested in putting together any type of memorial for Charles', though we knew *not* doing so would not only look odd to the police, but would be unfair to the children. Thus, for their sake, we decided to organize a service.

On the day of the service, we all woke early and dressed in our finest black clothes, making our way to the church in a black towncar. Nobody uttered a word for the entirety of the ride. Finally, after a crushingly long 45 minutes, we arrived at the church. Making our way into the waiting area, Valerie spoke for the first time.

"Austin, why don't you take your sister and go sit down." Valerie said, softly. "Your uncle and I will do the greetings. You don't need to worry about that." Austin and Madeleine made their way through the large mahogany doors, into the chapel. I waited until they were out of earshot before speaking.

"Do you think a lot of people will come?" I asked Valerie.

"Charles did know a lot of people." She began. "I don't know how many of them actually liked him, though."

"What about his family?" I asked. I had never met them.

"Well, his parents are dead." She said. "As for his siblings, I'm sure Rebecca and Jacob will be here. I spoke to both of them and they said they were going to try their best to make it. I would highly doubt Jacqueline shows up though. Nobody's spoken to her in years, and even before that, I don't think they ever spoke much. Especially her and Charles."

Over the next hour, a relatively large number of people arrived at the church. Acquaintances, coworkers, business associates, and friends of Valerie's all lined up to shake her hand, or offer a stiff hug, as they struggled to muster up a kind word to say about her dead husband. Sure enough, Charles' eldest siblings, Rebecca and Jacob showed up, though they were the last to arrive. We exchanged introductions quickly as they made their way into the chapel.

"Seems kind of odd they'd show up so late." I said.

"The whole family's a bit odd." Valerie replied.

"Speaking of odd family..." I began. "I'm surprised mother didn't show up."

"Are you really surprised?" Valerie asked.

"At the very least, I would've thought she'd show up to make an insensitive comment or two."

We made our way into the chapel. Valerie and I sat in the front row, alongside Madeleine and Austin. Charles' siblings sat in the pew behind us. The service was quick and rather unemotional, though Rebecca did utter a faint sniffle about halfway through.

As the service came to an end, the guests began to clear out rather quickly. Before long, the church was empty once more. "I'm going to run to the restroom." Valerie began. "Why don't you guys go wait in the car?" She made her way out of the chapel, down the hall, and into the ladies room.

"Austin, go ahead and take your sister to the car." I said. "I'm going to wait behind, I don't want to leave your mother alone." Austin nodded, taking his sister's hand in his. The two of them exited the chapel and, eventually, I heard as the door to the church close behind them. I stayed seated in the pew, peering at the stained glass windows around me, my mind racing a hundred miles per hour.

Several seconds later, I heard the door to the church open once more. The sound of stiletto heels clicking against the hard tile floor inched closer and closer. I stood from the pew, moving towards the back of the chapel. Swinging open the mahogany doors that separated the chapel from the waiting area, I began to speak.

"I'm sorry, the service is..." I began, before stopping mid-sentence.

There she was, standing in front of me, after all these years. Wearing a knee-length, skin-tight black dress, a mink stole resting around her shoulders. Her long, auburn hair fell beautifully over her smooth face. The mother of my child.

"Carlotta...." I said, shocked. "What are you doing here?"

"Jackson!" She said, running towards me and embracing me in a tight hug. "I was hoping you'd be here." I pulled away from her, sharply.

"Carlotta, of course I'm here." I said, incredulously. "Why are YOU here?"

Before she could answer, Valerie's voice called out from behind me. I hadn't even heard her return.

"Oh my God." Valerie began. "You actually came." I looked at both of them for several seconds before speaking once more.

"What is going on here?" I stammered. "You two know each other?"

"We've never actually met before." Valerie said.

"Carlotta, what is going on?" I asked. "How do you know my sister?"

Before she could answer, Valerie spoke once more.

"Her name isn't Carlotta." Valerie said. "This is Jacqueline, Charles' sister."

CHAPTER EIGHT: All My Children

"What did you just say?" I asked, incredulously.

"This is Jacqueline." Valerie replied. "This is Charles' sister."

There was a long, intense silence in the room, before Carlotta finally broke the tension. "You must have me confused with somebody else." She cooed, her eyes locking with mine.

"Yes…" I began, the word sputtering out clumsily. "Yes, I must."

"But didn't I hear you say you were hoping Jackson would be here?" Valerie asked, confused.

"You did…" Carlotta replied, quickly. "I'm a fan of his work, is all."

"Oh." Valerie said, clearly irritated.

"So, I missed the service?" Carlotta asked, her eyes softening.

"I'm afraid so." Valerie replied.

"Do you mind if I have a moment" Carlotta began. "With my brother?"

"Be my guest." Valerie replied, moving towards the door. "It was lovely to finally meet you, Jacqueline. Come on, Jackson, let's go home."

"Actually..." I began. "I'm going to catch up with you later. I have a couple of errands that I need to run."

"Oh." Valerie replied, clearly surprised. "Okay then. I'll see you later."

With that, she made her way through the door and out of the church. I watched as she walked slowly down the steep concrete steps. The driver quickly made his way to the rear of the car, opening the door and helping my sister inside. A moment later, they were gone. I turned to face Carlotta. "What the fuck was that?"

"You weren't exactly thinking on your feet." She mused. As she spoke, she made her way to a bench located on the far side of the room. Flinging her fur off of her shoulders; she quickly sat, removing her tall stiletto heels. "I remember you being much smoother than that." She laughed.

"I'm sorry if I was a little shocked to see you." I said, sarcastically, moving towards her.

"Well, are you happy to see me?" She asked, devilishly.

"Not exactly." I replied, avoiding her gaze.

"Well, that's no fun!" She said.

"You have some serious explaining to do." I replied, icily.

"You want to know why I'm here?"

"I want to know why you're here. I want to know why Valerie thinks your name is Jacqueline. Most of all, I'd like to know how you're my dead brother-in-law's fucking sister.

"Well, I didn't know back then, if that's what you're asking." She said, smiling at me softly and motioning for me to sit next to her. I sat down, still averting my eyes from hers.

"You didn't?"

"No. I promise you that." She said, reaching out to touch my hand. I quickly recoiled.

"Then how did you find out?"

"I never had a relationship with Charles, or any of my siblings. I hardly knew them and what I did know, I didn't exactly like."

"But I knew your brother!" I said, more loudly than I intended. "Adam was my best friend! Are you telling me that he's Charles' brother, too?"

"No!" She began. "Adam is my brother on my mother's side. Charles, Rebecca and Jacob, they're my siblings on my father's side. Like I said, I hardly knew them."

"So you expect me to believe you just happened to wind up in my life, and you had no idea that our siblings were married to each other?"

"I really had no clue, Jacky." She said, touching my hand once more. This time I didn't shrug her off. "I didn't know until years after the last time I saw you, I swear. I didn't find out until Charles' reached out to me."

"He did what?" I asked, shocked. We made eye contact for the first time in several moments.

"A couple of years after…." She began, her voice cracking. There were tears in her eyes. "After I had our daughter. He reached out, said he wanted a relationship. He sent me a bunch of family photos and there you were. I was shocked."

"That doesn't make any sense." I said, standing. I moved towards the window.

"You know I've always had a strained relationship with my family." I began, pausing for a moment to gather my thoughts. "Until about a month ago, I hadn't spoken to Valerie or Charles in years. It doesn't make sense that he would be including me in any pictures, let alone ones he sent to you."

"Think about it, Jacky."

I turned to face her. "Do you think he knew?"

"That we had a child together?" She asked. "I don't know, did he?"

"He knew I had a daughter, obviously, but I never told him who her mother was. Not so much as a first name."

"Well I certainly didn't tell him!" She said, firmly. "I thought about it, but I didn't want it to complicate things for you, or for our daughter. I left her with you. I gave up my rights to be her parent. I didn't want to do anything that was going to rock the boat. Like I said, he reached out to me, said he wanted to get to know me, to help me out. He sent pictures, of his family, his wife and children, you. But he didn't say anything at all about us."

"He has to have known. It doesn't make sense otherwise." I said, my mind and heart both racing.

"Why wouldn't he have said anything? Or done anything? It's been six years and he never mentioned a thing."

"What kind of relationship did you have with him after that?" I asked.

"We kept in touch. Phone calls here and there. He sent me money a couple of times when I was in some trouble, but nothing beyond that.."

"Don't fucking call me that." I grimaced, more harshly than I'd intended.

"I've always called you that." She replied.

"You don't get to waltz in here after all these years and hit me with pet names, Carlotta. Oh, wait, that's not even your name."

"It is!" She said, loudly. "It is my name! I haven't been Jacqueline for a very long time."

"You just changed your name? What kind of con were you running?
She paused, her eyes locked with mine. Suddenly, she was blinking back tears.

"You know my ex husband is a monster, Jackson. That's why I changed my name. I didn't want him to find me."

"Oh so that story was true?" I said, coldly, my words clearly stinging her.

"I'm not a liar, Jackson. I'm a lot of things, but I'm not a liar."

"Even if I do believe you. Even if I can stretch my mind so far to believe that you had no clue who I was, or that Charles' didn't know about us. Or any story you've ever told me, for that matter. Even if I believe those things, it doesn't give you the right to show up here."

"Jacky..." She began.

"God DAMN it, Carlotta!" I shouted, cutting her off. "Stop. You won't charm your way back into my life. You are a user – a manipulative, money hungry user. I want nothing to do with you."

"That's not true." She said, wiping the tears from her eyes.

"It is!" I replied, my voice cracking as tears formed in my own eyes. "I loved you, and you left. The minute I didn't have anything to offer you anymore, you left. You were the first to go."

"I'm sorry, Jackson." She replied, genuinely. "I was wrong. I was scared."

"Of what?" I shouted back. "What could you possibly have been scared of?"

"Ruining your life."

"What does that even mean?" I asked, incredulously.

"I knew that I was pregnant, Jackson, before everything happened with the money. I knew that if I was honest, that if I told you straight away, that you'd stay, that you'd give up your whole life for me." Tears flowed from her beautiful brown eyes, makeup cascading down her pale white cheeks.

"You don't get to do that." I replied. "You don't get to pretend that what you did was nice, that you were protecting me. You can't just tell me you left for my own good. I won't accept that. I can't. You broke me, Carlotta. Do you not understand that? You were the first person that I ever really believed loved me, and you threw that in my face. No, even worse, you threw it away like it was nothing. You don't get to come in here now and pretend it was some noble act."

"I know that what I did was wrong." She said, desperately. She moved, slowly, across the room between us. As she reached me, she brought her cool hands to my face. My heart jumped at her touch. Holding me like this, we locked eyes once more.

"I know that I'm not a good person." She said. "I'm not making excuses. I'm not saying what I did was right. I just want you to know that that's why I left. It had nothing to do with the money. I was trying to spare you, to save you. I thought it was better for you to think of me as a monster. I wanted to you to hate me, so that you could get away from me." I turned away from her once more.

"But you told me." I began. "A few months later, you told me you were pregnant. If all of what you just said was true, why do that?"

"I realized you had a right to know your daughter." She began. "You deserved that. I should've realized it sooner, but I didn't. I knew that I couldn't raise her, and I thought maybe you, or your family, could. I don't know, but I knew you deserved the chance to at least make the decision for yourself."

"This is all just...." I began.

"I know." She said, cutting me off. She reached out, grabbing my shoulder. I turned to look at her.

"So you do all this. You run away, you leave me, for whatever reason. Then you dump our kid on me and I never hear from you, for eight years, and now you show up out of nowhere, expecting me to believe your stories. Why? What do you want?"

"I wanted to come to Charles' funeral. We weren't close, but like I said, he helped me out. I hoped to see you here, that we could talk."

"About what?" I snapped. "What is the point of any of this?"

"I know you gave our daughter up for adoption. I know you did what you thought was best for her, but-"

"No!" I shouted, quietly. "No, absolutely not. We are not doing this. I can't. I won't. I'm not talking to you about this. It's not open for discussion. Our daughter is living happily with the only family she's ever known. She has no clue that we exist, and that's not going to change." She didn't say anything for a long moment.

"We can discuss this later." She replied. She moved towards the other side of the room, grabbing her things and walking past me, towards the exit.

"I will be in New York, at least for a while." She said. "I'll be in touch, Jacky." She turned, grabbing the doorknob, before stopping. "Oh!" She said, her tone changing. "I almost forgot, I have something for you." She opened her bag, pulling from it a large manila envelope.

"What is this?" I asked, confused, as I took the envelope from her.

"I'm not sure." She replied. "A man showed up at my hotel room this morning and asked me to give it to you, should I run into you here. It was rather odd, really."

"Thank you, I guess." I said, eyeing the package suspiciously.

She didn't respond. Instead, she moved towards me once more. Reaching her right hand towards me, she lifted my chin slightly, our eyes locking again. She leaned in, kissing me slowly. As the kiss ended, she smiled at me and spoke once more.

"I'll see you soon, Jacky."

I stared for a long moment at the package, before opening it. A small note fell from the envelope to the ground. Bending down, I picked up the note and unfolded it. It read:

"Never forget.
-Charles"

My hands began shaking. Slowly, I reached into the envelope, removing the remainder of its contents. I could feel my heart drop.

The following few days whizzed by in a blur, the police continuing to come and go from the house. Our story seemed to be holding up, though they questioned us repeatedly, asking the same handful of questions a hundred different ways. Last they told Valerie, they seemed to believe that an outside intruder had killed Charles.

"The den window appears to have been broken from the outside." Detective Lewis had told her. "We believe, at this time, that this may be how the killer entered, and exited, your home. Your husband was a powerful man, Mrs. Sinclair - he had a lot of enemies." It all seemed just a bit too good to be true.

I stood, slowly, from my bed. Peering at the alarm clock located on my bedside table, I realized that it was nearly noon.

"Shit." I mumbled. This had become my life over the past several days. I was constantly up all night, my mind churning over and over the events of the past few weeks. Charles, Carlotta, the envelope - it was all too much.

Stretching, I moved towards the door to my room, swinging it open. After a moment, I heard voices coming from Austin's room. Moving closer, I could hear Austin as he spoke to Madeleine.
"I miss Daddy." Madeleine said, her voice strained from crying.

"I know." Austin replied, softly. "I know you do, Maddie." I moved closer to the room, standing in Austin's doorway as he embraced his younger sister. Several seconds later, we made eye contact.

"Hey." He said. At that, Madeleine looked up, quickly.

"Uncle Jackson!" She shouted, running to hug me. I still wasn't used to the type of endearing, consuming love that comes from a child. I had hardly paid her the attention she deserved, yet here she was, so excited to see me.

We hugged for a long moment. Finally, she released her small arms from around my neck. She looked me in the eye for several seconds, her face scrunched in confusion.

"Uncle Jackson." She began. "Are you my Daddy now?" I felt the air leave my lungs.

"Wha..." I started. "No, no sweetie. I'm your uncle. Always."

"Oh." She replied.

"Why do you ask that?" I asked.

"Well, now that Daddy's gone, it's just Mommy. My friends all have a Mommy and a Daddy. If I just have a Mommy, what happens? "

"What do you mean?" I asked her.

"Will she still have time to take care of me?" She asked.

Before I could stop myself, I felt the tears in my eyes once more. I picked her up and pulled her into a tight hug.

"Of course she will, sweetie." I said, loosening the hug to look her in the eye once more. "We are all going to take care of you. Me, Austin, you, and your mommy, we're a family."

"Okay." She said, smiling a little. "I love you, Uncle Jackson!"

"I love you, too, kiddo." I said, smiling back. I set her down, and she exited the room.
"How are you holding up?" I asked Austin, after Madeleine was out of earshot.

"I'm holding up." He replied, unconvincingly.

"You know you can always talk to me." I said. He nodded.

"We're not done talking about the things we were talking about before, either." I said. "We have a lot to discuss." He nodded once more.

It caught my eye as I turned to leave the room. Peeking out from underneath Austin's bed was a silk handkerchief. Embroidered in large blue letters along the bottom of the cloth were the letters "C.A.S." - the initials of Charles Allen Sinclair.

Underneath Austin's bed lay his father's handkerchief.

Covered in blood.

I continued making my way out of the room, shutting the door gently behind me. What had I just seen? Why was it there? I didn't have much time to process however, as before my mind could wrap itself around what it had just seen, I heard as Valerie called out to me from the foyer.

"Jackson?" She said, loudly enough that she knew I would hear.

"Yes?" I said, making my way to the top of the staircase, where I could see her standing, fully dressed in the foyer.

"Get dressed." She said. "We have to go see mother."

I didn't question her, as I knew that Valerie going out of her way to see our mother meant that there must be a valid reason. I turned, making my way back to my room. I quickly threw on a sweater and jeans, and made my way downstairs.

Valerie and I didn't speak much as we sat in the back of the town-car, making our way to our mother's hotel. "What's this all about?" I asked, softly, after about ten minutes of silence.

"I have no clue." She replied, earnestly. "But mother phoned and said we needed to visit her. I of course said no, but she insisted." I nodded and turned to stare out the window. What could our mother want now?

After another five or so minutes, we arrived at the hotel at which our mother was staying. We made our way into the lobby, approaching the large, green marble counter that sat directly next to the lobby's grand staircase.

"Hello." Valerie said. "I'm here to see my mother, Tabitha Arrington." The young man behind the counter smiled faintly as he began entering our mother's name into the computer in front of him.

"Ah, yes." He replied. "Your mother is expecting you. Room 2304."

"Thank you." Val said, quickly, as she turned to make her way towards the elevator.
Upon reaching the 23rd floor, we quickly exited the elevator to our right, following the sign that read "Rooms 2300-2320, this way". After about three steps, we arrived at our mother's room.

"Here goes nothing." Val said, as she raised her arm, knocking three times on the heavy wooden door.

"Coming." Our mother's voice called out, coarse and distant. Several moments later, the door finally swung open, but it wasn't our mother that stood in front of us.

"Aunt Charlene." I said, shocked. "Oh my God!"

Before I knew what I was doing, I had flung myself past Valerie and into my Aunt's arms. "It's so good to see you!!" I said, my voice cracking. I felt tears welling up in my eyes, but these tears were different. They were happy.

"I haven't seen you in so long." I said, wiping my eyes. "Not since you moved to England, what, 15 years ago?"

"Sixteen." She replied, smiling at me softly.

"Hello, Aunt Charlene." Valerie said, moving in for a brief hug. They had never been close.

"Hello, darling." Aunt Charlene replied.

"Well, is anyone going to say hello to me?" My mother asked, sarcastically.

Moving past Aunt Charlene and into the suite, I laid eyes on my mother for the first time in weeks. There she was, sitting next to the large, bay window. Dressed in a long, silk nightgown, she held a cigarette in one hand, and a drink in the other.

"Hello, mother." I said, coolly, remembering that she was sick.

"Hello." She said, without looking up at me.

"Is this why you wanted to see us?" Valerie asked, confused.

Standing from her chair, our mother turned to look at Valerie and I for the first time since we had entered. Slowly, she took a sip of her drink, before setting it down on the table next to her.

"I needed Jackson to come here, and I knew he wouldn't do so without you." She replied, icily.

"What?" I began. "Why me?"
"I thought it was important that you reunite with your Aunt Charlene, dear."

"That's..." I began. "Why? What's the catch?"

"Why don't you tell him, Charlene?" She said, cackling softly.

I turned to face my Aunt once more. She stood there, looking back at me for a long moment. There was a smile on her face, but her eyes were an odd mixture of sad and nervous.

"Well..." Said our mother.

"What is it?

"Oh, fine then!" Said our mother. "I'll say it if she won't!"

"Say what?" I asked, confused.

Taking a puff of her cigarette, our mother drew closer to me. Standing not two inches away, she blew the smoke into my face, laughing.

"This bitch" She said. "Is your mother."

CHAPTER NINE: Loving

I stood there for a long moment without saying a word. "What did you just say?"

"I don't think I stuttered." Tabitha said, her mouth contorting into a small, devilish smile.

With that, Tabitha pointed one of her bony, heavily ringed fingers towards the woman standing just several feet away from her. Another liar.

Aunt Charlene stood there in utter silence, her eyes aimed firmly at her feet. Her face was pale, her brow furrowed. After several long seconds, she finally raised her eyes to mine.

"Jackson..." She began. I turned my back to her and made my way to the opposite side of the room. I reached the suite's kitchen and immediately flung open the small refrigerator, knocking out several small bottles of liquor, loudly.

I reached into the refrigerator, grabbing a small bottle of vodka. Unscrewing the lid as quickly as possible, my hands brought the bottle to my lips. The liquor stung as it slid down my throat.

Kneeling to the ground, I gathered the fallen bottles in my hands as I felt my own tears begin to slide down my cheek. I let go of the bottles, barely noticing as they clinked to the ground. Slowly, I sat, my back pressing against the cupboard behind me, my legs pressed against the cold, hard tile floor.

"Why?" I said. "Why?" I repeated, my voice drained and distant.

For a moment, nobody replied. Finally, Valerie made her way across the room. I opened my eyes for the first time, looking up at my older sister. She kneeled down next to me, and spoke.

"Why don't we get out of here?" She said softly, as she placed her hand on my shoulder. "You don't need to deal with this right now. We can do this later." Her voice was quiet, almost a whisper. "No." I said.

Tabitha and Charlene continued to stand in poisonous silence at the other side of the room, looking neither at each other, nor Valerie and I. Slowly, I pushed myself up from the floor. Grabbing the edges of the marble counter top, I stabilized myself for a moment. My mind was racing, a thousand thoughts whirling amongst a million emotions as I moved to the opposite side of the room.

"Why?" I said, turning to move towards them.

"Why, what?" Charlene asked.
"Why did you lie to me? Why did you abandon me?"

"It was very complicated, Jackson..." She started.

"And where did the complication start?" I asked, coolly. "When you fucked your sisters husband?" There was a long pause.

"Jackson..." She said, her voice shaking slightly. "It was more complicated than that."

"Fine." I said, agitated. "Un-complicate it for me. Explain to me what is complicated about you sleeping with your sister's husband, then dumping the kid to play the role of "cool aunt" for as long as it suited you."

"Your father and I…" She began, pausing to breathe in, intently. "Your father and I were in love." Tabitha winced ever so slightly.

"How beautiful." I replied, sarcastically.

"I'm not defending myself." Charlene replied, defensively. "You asked me to explain, and I am."

"Go on, then." I said, sitting in the plush arm chair near the window.

"It wasn't right. We shouldn't have acted on our feelings, but I don't regret it, because it brought you into this world, Jackson."

"Oh, please." I said. "Don't come here and spit platitudes like that at me. You don't even know me, to say something like that."

"I stayed for as long as I could, Jackson."

"What does that even mean?" I asked.

"Your father and I, we had been together for several years - just over three, to be exact. Then things got bad, and they got bad very quickly. Your mother found out what we were doing and, justifiably, was very, very angry, and very, very hurt. I didn't know what to do. I left town, but your mother followed me."

"What? Why?" I asked.

"Because I was stupid." Tabitha said, speaking for the first time in several moments. "Because she was my sister, and I thought, my best friend. I tracked her down, and found her knocked up with my husband's kid. She didn't even have the courtesy to get a goddamn abortion." Her words stung, lingering in the air like a dark cloud.

"I didn't think I would see your mother again. I never thought she would come after me. I thought I could raise you on my own." Charlene said, wiping her eyes.

"So, why didn't yofu? Why couldn't you?" I asked.

"When your mother found me, I was very pregnant. There was no lying myself out of that one. She knew that you were your father's child." I didn't reply. My whole body felt numb. Eventually, Valerie spoke in my place.

"So, what did you do, mother?"

"I told the bitch exactly what I thought of her." Tabitha replied, harshly. "And then I left. I went home, to my husband, and to you, my daughter. I thought that would be the last of it."

"But..." Valerie began.

"But your father figured it out." Tabitha said, cutting Valerie off.

"How?" I asked, not looking at any of them.

"I suppose your father was worried about his mistress, thought I was going to do something to her, which, really, would have been justified. He had me followed, and when I went to see her, the cat was out of the bag."

"So what did he do?" I asked.

"He insisted that he have a relationship with you. That's the first thing he said, that he wanted to know his son. I couldn't talk him out of it. He wouldn't hear of it." She paused, trying to hide the emotion that had crept into her voice. Fumbling through her purse, she quickly lit another cigarette, turning her back to us.

"He came to see me." Charlene said, glancing almost lovingly at her sister. "I told him I wanted to raise the baby alone, that I thought that was best, but he wouldn't hear of it."

"I don't understand that." I replied. "He never paid me any attention growing up. He was never even around."

"I think it was more the principle of it, for him." Charlene said.

"So, what? You just agreed to dump me off on them?"

"No." She began. "We argued about the situation for months, right up until I gave birth to you. Then I did what I thought was best. Your father was insistent that he would have a relationship with you even if I raised you on my own, and I thought that would be too confusing to you. It didn't seem like the kind of situation you explain to a child."

"Well, the alternative was no childhood, and a lifetime of abuse. So, thank you." I replied.

"I didn't know that!" Charlene replied. "I knew my sister could be difficult, but I had never seen that hardened version of her. She offered to raise you as her own, and I don't know why she did that. I don't know what her motives were, but I thought that was what would be best for you to have a stable family, to have a mother and father and sister and a home. It seemed so much safer than the alternative."

"If you'd stuck around past, say, my 9th birthday, you'd have known that wasn't the case." I said.

"I told you, I stayed as long as I could." She replied, softly.

"Yeah, and I still don't know what the hell that's supposed to mean."

"I loved being your aunt. I loved that I was allowed to have a relationship with you. I loved that I felt like you relied on me, and trusted me." She said, smiling softly.

"I DID rely on you. I DID trust you." I exclaimed.

"I couldn't respect the boundary anymore, Jackson." She started. "I couldn't just be your Aunt Charlene. I couldn't deal with the choice I made. The older you got, the more

I wanted to be your mother, and the more I regretted the choice I had made. I couldn't imagine the thought of destroying the only life you'd known, so I left."

"I suppose it's easier to look back and apologize and make excuses for yourself, than it would've been to actually stick around and make an effort." I replied.

She didn't respond.

"You know, at least Tabitha stayed." I began, pausing for a moment. "I don't know what's worse - The type of love that causes someone to treat a child so cruelly, or the type of love that causes you to abandon your own child. Maybe I'm a fool, maybe a lifetime of fucked up relationships has made me an idiot, but at least she stayed."

"I'm sorry."

"Maybe we should go." Valerie said, moving towards me. "This is a lot to deal with, Jackson. You don't need to do it now."

"Did you know?" I asked, standing to meet my sister halfway.

"What?"

"Did you know?" I repeated. "Did you know that she was my mother?"

"No!" She replied, quickly cutting me off. "I had no idea. I swear to you."

"She didn't know." Tabitha said, softly, though her voice was cold.

"Fine." I said. "Then why are you telling me? Why now? Why not weeks ago?"

"I didn't tell you then…" She began, turning to face me. "Because I thought maybe I would spare you the pain."

I didn't respond.

"Surprise, surprise!" She spat, laughing. "The bitch had a heart for a moment!"

"So what changed your mind?"

"I heard about what happened." Charlene interjected, before Tabitha could reply. "I knew that it was time that I came home to my family. When I got here, Tabitha told me that she told you the truth. I thought she should tell you the truth."

"Well, great." I replied. "A real favor you've done me here."

"I thought you deserved to know." She replied, softly.

"Only 26 years too late." I shouted. "Come on, Val. Let's go."

As we made our way towards the door to the suite, Val turned around to speak once more.

"Always good to see you, mother…." She said, her voice flat, her face tight with emotion. "And thank you for coming to my husband's funeral to support me and my children in such a hard time."

She turned, once more making her way towards the door. Our mother's words stopped her short.

"I didn't think it would be appropriate, seeing as my last encounter with the bastard was quite ugly. Which, pretty much sums up my feelings about that asshole, in general."

"What are you talking about?" Valerie asked. "Did you and Charles have an argument?"

Our mother looked at her for several seconds, taking a puff of her cigarette once more before speaking.

"Don't worry about it."

With that, we left.

As we reached the lobby of the hotel building, Valerie quickly removed her cell phone from her purse and phoned the driver, letting him know we were ready to be picked up.

"Actually, Val…" I began. "I've got somewhere I need to go."

"Where are you going?" She replied, her voice dripping with concern. "Is there something you need to tell me?"

"No." I replied, smiling. "I'm just going to see someone. A friend, I guess."

"Alright." She replied. "But be careful."

She leaned in, kissing me softly on the cheek, before exiting the lobby. I watched as she entered the long black town car that was waiting for her. As the car pulled off, I reached into my pocket, grabbing my own cell phone. I dialed quickly, raising the phone to my ear as it began to ring. On the third ring, she answered.

"Jules?" I asked, softly. "It's Jackson. Can I see you?"

We agreed to meet at a small diner not far from the hotel I was already at. I made my way across the lobby, onto the busy Manhattan street. When I arrived at the diner several moments later, Jules was already there, waiting for me at a small table near the window.

"Jackson!" She said, standing from her chair to wave. I made my way across the small restaurant. As I reached the table, I did something I rarely, if ever, do.

I hugged her. Tightly. I could tell she was surprised by the hug, though after several seconds, her arms wrapped tightly around my waist. "Are you okay?" She whispered, as the hug broke.

"I don't know." I said, taking a seat on the small wooden chair across the table from her. "I guess I should be used to these kinds of things by now."

"What kinds of things?" She asked, her face scrunched with confusion.

For the next twenty minutes, we sat, as I told her, in new detail, everything that had happened since my return to New York - from my attempt at suicide, to Charles' murder, to Carlotta showing up. I told her everything. Almost everything.

"Wow…" She said, her voice filled with shock. The server arrived to deliver our food. "That's a lot to take in."

"It's a lot to live." I replied, chuckling.

"I'm sorry you've had to deal with all of that, Jackson." She said, reaching across the table to touch my hand, gently.

"Thanks." I said, squeezing her hand.

"What are you feeling?" She asked.

"Right now?" I began. "I'm mostly just pissed off. I'm so sick of everyone in my life lying to me. I don't know what I ever did to deserve this fucked up family."

"You didn't do anything, Jackson." She replied. "Sometimes we get dealt a shitty hand, but that doesn't mean it's your fault."

"I just don't get it." I said, ignoring her sentiment. "How can someone just pawn her child off like that? And why?"

"Didn't you say they were in love?"

"So that makes it okay?" I replied, incredulously.

"No…" She started. "No, it doesn't, but people have done a lot of crazy things under the guise of love. I'm not saying what she did was right, but she also wasn't the one who took a vow. Love is a complicated game, you know that."

"She owed her sister more than that. Don't you think?"

"I don't know their relationship, and maybe you don't either." She said.

"I just don't understand." I replied, playing with the food on the plate in front of me.

"I'm surprised to hear you defending your mother, though. Maybe that's something good that can come from all of this – a new understanding of the way she operates."

"Well it certainly makes me understand why she's so bitter. Charlene made her that way. And my father, too, I suppose."

"Nobody MAKES anybody do anything…" She replied. "People are who they are. Sure, the actions of others may bring certain traits out, but Charlene, or your father, they didn't MAKE her that way. They didn't MAKE her treat you that way. That's a choice she made."

"So whose side are you on here?" I replied, more angrily than intended. "Because you seem to be defending everybody except me."

"I'm on your side, of course." She said, smiling earnestly at me from across the table. "I just want you to think about this from every possible angle. This is a lot to take in, from a lot of different people, and you have to consider each of their motivations before you decide how to feel."

"So what do you suggest? That I just forgive my Aunt Charlene and accept that she had good intentions? I'm not even sure I believe that."

"Why wouldn't you?"

"I don't understand how you can just leave a child, when you know they're not in a good environment. Maybe that makes me a hypocrite, because I gave up my own daughter, but I never would have left her with someone that I didn't think would love her and give her the best life possible."

"I think your aunt did the same." She replied, softly.

"How so?" I replied, incredulously. "She saw what was going on, and her answer was to run!"

"Yes, but that was long after she made her decision!" She said. "When you were a baby, she left you with the family she thought could give you the best home. Maybe she changed her mind years later, and maybe she shouldn't have left then, either. She was doing what she thought was best for you. She had made her decision, and she didn't feel she had a right to intervene. I don't think she was being malicious, Jackson. I truly don't."

I paused for a moment, taking a sip of my water as her words settled in.

"How can you be so sure?" I asked, sincerely.

"Let me rephrase this as a question: What reason do you have NOT to believe her?"

"Other than the fact that my whole life has, in general, been a big lie?"

"Seems pretty shitty to just expect everything to be a lie."

"Maybe we've just led different lives" I began. "But for me, it's just easier to expect the worst. It's easier to always expect that people will fuck you over." She looked at me intently for several, long, seconds.

"That's terrible, Jackson." She replied.

"Oh, don't cry." I said, a lump rising in my own throat.

"I know we don't know each other that well, but sometimes you don't have to know someone for a long time to have a connection with them. I care about you, and I'm going to show you that you're wrong, that your way of thinking isn't right."

"I hope you can." I said, smiling at her as I blinked back tears.

"I know this is absolutely the most inopportune moment to leave" She began, chuckling as she wiped her eyes. "But I have to go to work! I'm so sorry!"

"It's okay." I said, as we both stood from the table. "We'll do this again soon?"

"Please." She said, smiling as she wrapped her arms around me in a tight hug.

We made our way out of the diner together, waving with a smile as we went in separate directions. I glanced down at my watch, shocked to realize how late it had gotten. I began heading towards Valerie's house when I noticed a small bar across the street.

I sat at the bar for several hours, thinking about everything that had happened. I was too distracted to even drink as much as I would've liked.

I made my way through the city streets, to Valerie's home. The walk took twice as long as it should've, but I was lost enough in my own thoughts not to notice. When I finally arrived at the house, I made my way, as quietly as possible, through the front door. It didn't matter, though, as somebody was awake in the living room.

"Hello?" I said softly, noticing the light shining from across the foyer.

"Hey". Austin replied, softly.

"Oh!" I said, relieved that it wasn't Valerie, there to lecture me. "What are you doing up?"

"Couldn't sleep." He replied.

"Let's go somewhere." I said.

"What?" He said, surprised.

"Let's go do something fun." I said.

"Like what?"

"I don't know. See a movie? Get some food? We'll figure it out." I said. "Do you have a car?"

"I don't even have a license." He replied, with a chuckle.

"Well, fuck." I said,. "I guess we're walking cause I'm fresh out of cab money."

"Actually" He began. "My dad had a car. Do you have a license?"

"Surprisingly enough."

"Great, I'll get the keys."

I was fine to drive, though. I'd only had two drinks. Or was it three?

We made our way to Charles' large, obnoxious Mercedes SUV. "My Dad would shit if he ever knew I was taking his car out." Austin said. "Not much he can do about it now, I guess." I chuckled at the joke, though it made me slightly uncomfortable.

We drove for several minutes, making small talk along the way.

"How is school?" I asked.

"It's fine, I guess." He replied. "I mean, I hate it, but it could be worse."

"That's the spirit." I said, with a laugh.

"How are you holding up?" I asked. "It's okay if you're not doing well right now." I glanced over at him. His head was turned towards the window, facing away from me. As we approached a stoplight, I slowed the car before turning right. The car behind me did the same, for the second time in as many blocks.

"Is it bad that I don't feel much of anything?" He asked.

"There's so much going on." I said. "It's a lot to process." He didn't reply, though he did turn his head to look at me, briefly. "What's on your mind?" I asked. "There's something you're not saying."

"Is anything ever going to be normal again?"

"Yes, but not the normal you're accustomed to. Things are going to be diff--" He cut me off before I could finish the sentence.
"Uncle Jackson, there's something I have to tell you." He whispered, his voice almost fearful. His face was pale and white, his eyes hollow.

Suddenly, I realized that the stoplight in front of me had turned red. I slammed on the brakes, but it was too late. Halfway into the intersection, the car screeched to a halt. An SUV headed in the opposite direction swerved, laying on their horn as they sped away. I looked up from the road, my heart racing.

"Are you okay?" I asked Austin.

But it was too late.

I felt the impact as the car slammed into us. I felt as our car left the ground, flipping onto its side.

My eyes opened, slowly, as I blinked them into focus. There was no pain, but I felt as blood dripped from my forehead, the taste filling my mouth.

Slowly, I reached down to unbuckle my seatbelt. Kicking my door open, I crawled from the overturned SUV, landing with a thud on the hard concrete.

"Austin?" I said, groggily. "Austin?" I repeated, much more loudly.

Crumpled on the pavement, his body limp and unmoving, he lay several feet from me. "Austin!" I screamed, running to his side, falling to the ground. He didn't move.
"Somebody help me!" I shouted.

I stood searching desperately for a passerby as I realized that my cellphone was no longer in my pocket. I noticed the SUV that had hit us - a large, white Range Rover, its hood smashed, almost to the windshield. "Are you okay?" I shouted to the driver. "Can you help us? Call someone!"

There was no reply. Desperate, I ran to the driver's side of the car, peering in.
Her body was motionless, her long auburn hair matted over her blood streaked face, resting against the hard, leather steering wheel.

Carlotta.

"Carlotta!" I screamed, reaching in to move the hair from her face. "Carlotta, wake up!" She moved, slightly, lifting her head towards mine. As she did, a small baggy of cocaine fell from her hand.

CHAPTER TEN: As the World Turns

My body froze. I turned my back from the SUV, on my heels, facing my nephew's motionless body once more. I made my way towards him. "Jackson?" She said, her voice groggy.

Turning to face her again, I watched as she sat upright, slowly. She pushed the blood-streaked hair from in front of her eyes and blinked rapidly as her gaze locked on me.

"What are you doing here?"

Her face was stricken with horror, her eyes growing wide as she spotted Austin, lying stiff on the ground. Before I could answer her first question, she began moving, frantically, in her seat. Her shaking hands fumbled to undo the seatbelt latch and, clumsily, she threw herself from the car and began towards me.

"Is that my nephew?" She asked, her voice coarse and broken.

I grabbed her firmly by the shoulders as she attempted to move past me. Steadying her, our eyes locked for several seconds.

"Carlotta." I began, pausing to take a panicked breath. "Carlotta, do you have a cell phone?"

"Yes." She stammered.

"I need you to give it to me. I need to call an ambulance."

Her face white and blank, she turned slowly and moved towards the SUV, now smoking from underneath its hood. She leaned in, slowly, grabbing her clutch purse from the passenger seat and removing her cell phone. As she turned to hand me the phone, I saw it again – the small baggy of cocaine.

She handed me the phone, its cold metal sending a tingle through my fingertips. She stumbled towards Austin as I clumsily dialed 911.

"Hello." I said, my voice flat, uneven, slightly in shock. "I need an ambulance."

As I hung up the phone, I moved towards Carlotta, who was now kneeling next to Austin. Her slender, white hand rested on his face, her crimson nails caressing his cheek softly.

"Carlotta."

She turned to look at me, her face streaked with makeup. She stood, reaching her hand out towards mine.

"Don't touch me." I said, recoiling from her.

"Jacky."

"Do you have any idea what you've done?"

"Jacky." She repeated.

"You're back on that shit, and that's your business. If you want to continue fucking up your life, go ahead, but you don't get to pretend to care about my nephew."

"He's my nephew, too." She replied, her eyes aimed intently at the ground.

"Don't you—" I began, but she cut me off.

"I'm not high, Jackson. I swear to you, I'm not."

"Bullshit!" I said, louder than I had intended.

"Jackson!" She pleaded, her eyes filling with tears. "I'm not. I swear to you on everything. I am clean."

"Then why do you have that shit?"

"I was at a party." She started, pausing to inhale sharply. "With some people I used to know. I didn't know they were still doing this shit, Jackson, I swear. They offered it to me, and I took it. I took it, but I didn't do it. I was about to blow 5 years of sobriety. I knew if I stayed, I would do it."

I didn't reply. Making my way towards Austin, I kneeled down on the wet pavement next to him, brushing his messy blonde hair aside with the back of my hand.

"I didn't see you." She continued. "I was distracted. It wasn't drugs. I swear to you, on our daughter, Jackson. I'm clean.

"Okay." I said, tears welling up in my eyes once more as I looked down at Austin. Before she could reply, the sound of sirens pierced the suffocating silence that had filled the air. They grew closer and closer.

"Jackson, I have to get out of here."

"What?" I said, incredulously.

"Jackson, that's not even my car! I took it, from the party. I'm driving a stolen car, and I don't even have a license. I'll go to jail Jackson."

"Carlotta, are you insane? You'll just explain to them what you explained to me."

"That I'm not on drugs?" She shouted back. "They can prove that with a simple test. It doesn't erase the myriad of other laws I've broken here. If I'm here when they get here, I am fucked. You have to tell them that you didn't see who was driving that car."

"Carlotta." I began.

"Jacky. Please. If you ever loved me...."

She looked at me, the way she always had, the way that had always worked. I looked at her for a moment, before glancing down, placing my hand on Austin's face once more.

The sirens grew louder and louder. I could just make out the rapid blue and red lights bouncing off of the dark pavement in the distance.

"Go." I said, softly, without looking at her.

Taking off her stiletto heels, she turned towards a nearby alley.

"Carlotta!" I called after her. She turned to look at me, barely visible from the entrance of the dark alleyway.

"I called from your cellphone."

"Pre-paid. Cash. Untraceable. You know me better than that." She said. With that, she was gone.

Time began whizzing by in a daze, making me feel somehow as if I was in slow motion and on fast-forward. The paramedics arrived, placing Austin's limp body on a long stretcher, loading him into the back of the ambulance as if he were a couch on college move in day.

"I have to go with him." I had mumbled, my head ringing, breathing staggered.

"Are you family?" The surly paramedic had asked. "You need to be examined yourself, let us take you in a separate..."

"No!" I barked, pushing past and making my way into the ambulance with Austin.

Now, here we were, an hour, or maybe two, after the accident. It took nearly a dozen attempts, both from the police and myself, before Valerie finally woke up and answered her phone. She'd always been a deep sleeper.

"Valerie." I had whispered, my voice trailing off on the last syllable of her name. "You need to get to Mercy

General. Right now. It's Austin. There's been an accident."

I'm sure there had been more to the conversation, but I couldn't remember it. There I sat, staring idly at my hands, my whole body numb.

"Mr. Arrington." Her voice was soft, smooth. "Mr. Arrington." She repeated.

"Yes?" I finally replied.

"We've taken your nephew into surgery, he's sustained some pretty serious injuries and unfortunately we weren't able to wait until your sister arriv--"

Before she could finish, the doors leading to the adjacent hallway burst open. Through them rushed Valerie, her hair matted and tangled, her face makeup-less and grey. "Where is my son?" She half shouted, her eyes instantly watering.

"Mrs. Sinclair..." The nurse began.

"Where is my son?" She repeated, more frantically this time, cutting the nurse off.

"He's been taken into surgery, ma'am."

"Surgery?" Valerie asked, her voice shaking. "For what?"

The nurse began explaining, something about his spine, about him hitting his head, about bleeding, about his brain. I didn't hear what she said, though, as my mind had focused on the tiny girl standing in the doorway.

She wore her favorite elephant pajamas, wrapped in a fuzzy pink blanket. My niece.

Her head was down, the edge of her blanket visibly wet from where she had nervously chewed it. I saw her small body tremble slightly as she choked on her own tears. "Madeleine." I said, softly. She looked up at me, her tiny face streaked with tears.

"Uncle Jackson!" She wailed, after a moment, as she ran towards me, collapsing in my arms. This little girl, who I had hardly given the attention she deserved, who loved me so much.

"It's okay, sweetie." I said, wiping the tears from her face and wrapping my arms around her tightly.

"Is Austin going to be okay?" She asked, her voice barely a whimper.

"Yes, baby." I said. "I promise you."

"Jackson." Valerie said, coldly, from several feet away.

"You sit right here for a minute, okay sweetie?" I said, guiding Madeleine into the cold plastic chair behind me, moving several steps towards my sister.

"Valerie." I began.

"You don't speak." She said, her voice icy. "What have you done to my son, Jackson? What have you done to my baby?" She raised her shaking hands to cover her face.

"Valerie, I - They came out of nowhere."

"How do you not see a giant SUV flying towards your car, Jackson? Tell me, how do you miss that?"

"You can ask the police, Valerie, I told them everything. I didn't see the car, I swear. They ran a red light. I didn't see them." My voice trailed off.

"Were you looking at the road?"

"I..." I stuttered.

"Were you looking at the GOD DAMN road, Jackson?!" She shouted, drawing the attention of several nearby nurses and passerby.

"No." I said, after a long moment, a softball sized lump rising in my throat. "I was talking to Austin, looking at him..."

"Talking to Austin. Looking at Austin." She spat. "AUSTIN! MY son, not yours. MY son, who you had no business taking out of MY home, without permission." I didn't say a word.

"Get out." She hissed after several long seconds.

"What?" I replied, my eyes meeting hers.

"I can't deal with you here. I can't have you here. I cannot look at you. Go home. Go somewhere. Get out."

"What about Madeleine?" I asked, softly.

"I'll take care of my daughter, thank you very much."
She said, and I knew the conversation was over. I turned
and made my way through the doors that my sister had
just burst through several moments beforehand. I felt
my heart sink as my body once again went numb. My
eyes started to blur. I felt myself falling, my right arm
grabbing the armrest on a nearby chair just as my knees
gave out. I pulled myself into the chair, cautiously,
clenching my eyes tightly shut.

"Are you okay, darling?" The voice was calm, almost a
whisper. I looked up at her, slowly, as my eyes came
back into focus.

"What are you doing here?" I asked.

"My son and grandson were in an accident, where else
would I be?" Tabitha replied, earnestly.

Son. The word stuck with me for a moment.

"But how did you even…" I began, my voice trailing off
as it dawned on me. "How did you know I was here?"
She paused for a moment, moving swiftly into the chair
next to mine. "When you left the hotel, I was afraid you
would do something reckless. I know a lot of people,
Jackson." She sighed.

"Someone from the hospital called you?" I asked. She
nodded.

"Maybe you know me better than I thought." I grimaced.
She smiled, absentmindedly, her mind clearly
elsewhere.

"Thank you, I guess."

"I'm sorry things went the way that they did." She said, reaching out to touch my hand, briefly. "You didn't need to find out like that."

"It's okay." I murmured.

"It's not." She said, standing and moving across the narrow hallway. She stood, her back to me, as she peered through a small window into the waiting area on the other side. "You deserved better than that." My throat went dry. I didn't reply for a long moment.

"How long have you been here?" I asked, desperate to change the subject.

"Over an hour, at least." She said, still not turning to face me. "I came as soon as I could. You were getting examined when I got here. You are okay, right?" She said, finally turning to look at me once more.

"I'm fine." I said.

Did she really care?

"And Austin...." She began. "He's in surgery?"

"Yes." I replied, tears suddenly flooding my eyes.

"What type of surgery?" She asked, her voice quiet. If I didn't know better, I would've sworn her words were filled with genuine concern.

"I don't know." I sputtered, unable to fight back the tears. "Something about his spine, I think...I don't know...It's my fault, though."

I buried my head in my hands, sobbing. She didn't reply for several long seconds. She placed her hand, gently, on my shoulder. I felt a small gust of wind as she sat in the chair next to me once more.

"Oh, Jackson..." She started, her voice cracking ever so slightly. "Don't do that. Don't blame yourself."

"But it's my fault!" I half shouted, half sobbed, my words almost incoherent. "It is!"

"What were you doing, you and Austin?" She asked, calmly.

"What do you mean?" I asked, looking at her through my tear-blurred eyes.

"Why were you with him? What were you doing?"

"We were just..." I began, pausing to breathe. "I just wanted to spend some time with him. I hadn't had the best day, obviously... I know he's been having a hard time. I just wanted to talk, about a lot of things..." My mind flashed to the bloody handkerchief.

"And you're punishing yourself for that?" She asked.

"What do you mean?" I replied, confused.

"You just wanted to spend time with your nephew. There's nothing wrong with that, Jackson."

"But look what happened!" I shouted. "He would never be here if it weren't for me! I should've never taken him out of the house. I should've never even suggested it."

"Were you drunk? Were you on drugs? Did you do it on purpose?" She asked, her voice steady and serious.

"What? No!" I said, defensively.

"Then it's not your fault, Jackson." She touched my hand once more.

I was silent for a long moment.

"I don't know." I finally replied, burying my head in my hands.

"One of the hardest things to learn in life, Jackson...." She began. "Is that everything we do, literally everything, is about choices. We make dozens, hundreds, hell maybe thousands of them every day. We choose to get out of bed in the morning. We choose what to wear, where to go, who to talk to. Those things seem small, and insignificant, but they're choices that we make. They impact our days and, sometimes, they turn into much bigger situations that require even more choices."

She paused again, reaching her hand out towards me, pulling my face gently from my hands and turning it towards her. Our eyes locked.

"When things like this happen, Jackson, the first thing we need to do is look back on the choices that we made.

Usually, we condemn them, wish we had done something differently, because the alternative will always be undiscovered. We'll never know what would have happened if you had chosen differently. You'll never know what the outcome would've been if you hadn't gotten in that car. Your mind is going to work overtime, trying to make you regret the choice you made. You didn't do anything wrong, Jackson. Your choice, to go out with Austin, it's over. It doesn't matter now. What matters now is focusing on Austin and whatever it takes to help him." I didn't answer immediately, as her words sunk in.

"I guess so."

She smiled at me for a moment, almost tenderly, before speaking again. "Now, that's not to say there aren't certain choices you should regret in life. I have a lot of those…" She said, trailing off before catching herself. "You didn't do anything wrong, Jackson." I didn't reply.

"Now, why don't you go back in there and get us an update?" She asked, breaking the silence.

"I can't."

"Why?"

"Valerie asked me to go home. She doesn't want to see me." I replied, trying my hardest not to start crying again.

"Oh." She replied, sharply.

"Yeah."

"Your sister loves you very much, Jackson." She said, her voice soft again. "She's upset and overwhelmed right now, but she loves you very much."

"She's the only one who does." I replied, chuckling cynically. "I probably fucked that up, too."

"That's not true." She replied, almost defensively. I looked at her, surprised.

"I…" She began, clearing her throat. "I love you, Jackson. I do."

She reached out, stroking my cheek softly with the back of her fingers.
"You know…" I said, standing. "You know, for so long I told myself that. I tried to believe it. I told myself you loved me, in your own fucked up way. At some point I stopped trying to trick myself into believing it. I think I was better off for that."

"I should have said it sooner." She replied, pausing. "I should have shown it."

"What was that you said about not regretting choices?"

"Like I said…" She started. "Some choices are worth regretting." For a brief second, her eyes glistened with tears.

"Well, it doesn't matter now."

"I know." She said, lowering her head.

"So I guess what matters is what happens going forward." She looked up at me, her eyes full with surprise.

"Now why don't you go in there and see Valerie instead of hiding out here?"

"Oh." She said, as if she'd had the wind knocked out of her. "Valerie doesn't want to see me."

"Maybe not." I said. "If you're nice to her, though, she'll appreciate you being here."

"I don't know."

"It's up to you." I said, turning to leave.

"Jackson!" She said, almost urgently, standing from her chair. I turned to face her.

"I never wanted anyone to hurt you. I know that sounds ridiculous coming from me. I never wanted you to get hurt the way that you have. You have no idea the lengths I would go to, the lengths I HAVE gone to, to protect you and your sister."

What did that mean?

Before I could ask, she turned and made her way through the doorway; towards the hallway I had left Valerie in just moments beforehand. I stood there, staring after her for several seconds.

I made my way home, not paying much attention to the route I took, or the things going on around me. It felt like hours before I finally reached the house, making my way directly up the stairs and to my room.

Opening the door, I stepped over piles of clothes, dirty and clean, collapsing onto the bed. Lying like this for several moments, my mind buzzed through the events of the night, as if it had all been some demented and dream.

Finally, I pulled myself up from the bed and made my way to the desk on the opposite side of the room. I pulled the top drawer open, dropping my wallet, along with Carlotta's cellphone, which I'd forgotten I still had, into it.

And then I noticed that it was missing, the envelope Carlotta had given me – the one from Charles.

A cold sweat instantly forming on my brow, I tore the desk apart looking for the envelope. It was nowhere to be found. I ripped through my dresser drawers, under the bed and mattress, pulled everything from my closet. Gone.

Like tiny flashes of lightening, the bright lights began flickering from the street below. I moved towards my window, parting the blinds ever so slightly. There they were.

Paparazzi.

Flying down the stairs, I tore through the foyer; swinging the front door open with such force, shaking it at its hinges. There they stood, reporters and photographers, huddled around the doorstep like a zoo exhibit. Had I left the front gate unlocked?

I opened my mouth - ready to tell them to fuck off - when I saw it. Clenched in the bony, hairy hands of the male reporter standing just three feet from me, was the envelope from Charles. My heart dropped.

Clenched between the envelope and his hand was a sheet of stiff, yellow paper.

"Mr. Arrington!" He shouted, though I was whispering distance from him. I didn't reply.

"Mr. Arrington!" He shouted again. I looked up at him, our eyes connecting for the first time.

"Is it true?" He asked. My eyes widened in horror.

"Is it true that your sister is raising your daughter?"

CHAPTER ELEVEN: Passions

I stood there, for what felt like hours, as the flash of the cameras blinded me. I stared, blankly at the reporter, a man in his 40's, with grey hair and deep wrinkles behind his unfeeling eyes.

"I..." I began, choking on my own words.

"Mr. Arrington! Is it true? Is it true that..." He repeated, though I was no longer listening.

"I..." I started again. "No comment." Slowly, I turned and made my way back into the foyer. I shut the door quickly behind me, my heart pounding in my chest.

"Mr. Arrington!! Could we just get a comment?"

"Jackson, just a yes or a no will do!"

I heard them shouting as the door clicked shut. I leaned backwards, pressing up against the cold metal of the front door. I slid to the floor, my face growing hot with tears. For several moments, I sat there. I sat there, thinking about what had just happened. Thinking about what this would mean: for me, for Valerie, for Madeleine. Who could have done this?

Carlotta. Did she know the truth?

After several more moments, I finally found the strength to stand from the floor. I turned, facing the door once more. Gently, I peeled back the curtains covering the window, just enough to see the flock of paparazzi still gathered at the doorstep. I knew that I had silently told them exactly what they wanted to know.

Turning quickly, before they could spot me, I made my way back upstairs and into my room. I stepped over the heaps of clothes I had dumped on the floor, and made my way towards the desk. I opened the top drawer, pulling out the cell phone I had placed there just a half an hour ago.

The phone didn't have a passcode, sliding unlocked with the simple swipe of a finger. Frantically, I began fumbling through the text messages and emails stored on the phone. Finally, I stumbled a cross an email confirmation for a hotel reservation:

> "Dear Ms. Winthrope,
>> We are writing to confirm your reservation at the Hotel Brynne. Attached are the details regarding your stay.
>
>> Best,
>>> The Hotel Brynne Staff"

I knew exactly where that was. Grabbing my coat off of the bed, I swiftly made my way out of the bedroom and down the stairs once more, skipping the top step and nearly falling. I grabbed the brass handle of the front door, flinging it open forcefully as I charged outside. The paparazzi still lingered outside the door.

"Mr. Arrington!" They shouted.

"Jackson!" They pleaded.

I paid them no attention as I pushed past them and through the front gate. I began pacing anxiously, hoping a cab would pass by soon. After several seconds, a bright yellow taxi turned the corner less than a block from where I stood. I hailed it frantically as I felt my phone begin vibrating in my pocket.

Fumbling, my hands still shaky, I removed the phone from my pocket and glanced quickly at the caller ID:

"Mother"

"I can't talk right now." I said, answering the phone as the cab stopped in front of me. "Hotel Brynne, please." I said to the driver as I sat down.

"Jackson, it's about Austin." She started.

"What about him?" I asked, nervously.

"He's out of surgery, but the doctors aren't saying much. I don't know anything else really, but I think you need to be here."

"Valerie doesn't want me there." I replied.

"But Austin will." She said, softly.

"I'm on my way." I said, hanging up the phone.

"Change of plans." I said to the cab driver. "I need to get to Mercy General, as quickly as possible."

Several moments later, we pulled up underneath the awning that covered the hospital's main entrance. I quickly swiped my card through the electronic reader, saying a prayer that there was enough on it to cover the ride. There was.

"Thank you." I mumbled frantically to the driver as I rushed out of the cab, heading towards the hospital's large, revolving glass door.

Once inside, I spotted the information desk on the other side of the lobby. "Hi, I need to find my nephews room, please. It's an emergency!" I half-shouted as I walked up to the desk.

"Okay sweetie." Said the kind-faced older woman behind the desk. "What's his name?"

"Austin Sinclair"

"Okay honey, it looks like he's still in recovery right now. From there, he'll either go to step down or the ICU, but you probably won't be able to see him for several hours."

"Okay." I said, my voice shaking. "Do you know where I could find my family then? Where would they be to wait for him?"

"My guess is that they're waiting to see him in the lounge on the 10th floor." She said. Exactly where I had left them.

"If they're not there, have the nurse at the desk up there page them for you." She said, but I was already walking away. I shouted a quick "Thank you!" over my shoulder as I approached the elevator.

As I stepped off of the elevator, I spotted my mother sitting across the large room, perched at the edge of the uncomfortable looking pleather couch. In the small pink chair across from her sat Valerie, her back to me. I made my way across the room, towards them.

"Any word...?" I said, softly, as I approached them.

Valerie looked up at me, her eyes red and puffy from hours and crying.

"What are you doing here?" She asked, breaking our eye contact to look down at the crumpled up tissue clutched firmly in her hand.

"I called him." Our mother said, her voice soft, yet firm.

"And why would you do that?" Valerie snapped, quickly.

"Because no matter what you think right now, you want him here. You do." Valerie didn't respond.

"Well" I started. "What's going on?"

"We don't know much..." Tabitha began.

"He's out of surgery." Valerie stated, cutting our mother off. "But he isn't awake. We won't know exactly how well the surgery went until he wakes up. If he wakes up..." Her voice trailed off as her eyes filled with tears. She raised the crumpled tissue to her eyes, blotting them softly.

"Oh, Val..." I said, reaching my hand forward and placing it on her shoulder.

Before she could answer, the sound of footsteps permeated the deafening silence of the waiting room. "I got everyone coffee. I wasn't sure what everyone liked so I just grabbed a bunch of cream and sugar." It was a female voice, one that I recognized.

Jules.

"Jules!" I said, incredulously. "What are you doing here?!"

"I didn't know you were here..." She began. "I saw in the system that you'd been admitted. I came as soon as my shift ended, but you were already gone. I thought the least I could do would be to get your family some coffee."

"Why?" I asked.

"I care about you Jackson. You weren't answering your phone, so I didn't know what else to do. I was going to go by your house and look for you after I dropped off the coffee."

"MY house." Valerie corrected her, sharply. Nobody spoke for several seconds.

"Thank you, Jules. It means a lot."

"You know what?" Val said, angrily, standing from her chair. "This is very sweet and all, but in case you forgot, my son is in a hospital bed fighting for his life. So if we're going to talk about anything, it should be that."

"I'm sorry, Val." I began. "I'll go. There's something I should take care of. Please keep me updated." She looked at me for the first time in several moments.

"Oh my God." She said, her voice thin, but full of anger. "You never change. Your nephew is in this hospital fighting for his life, because of YOU no less, and you can't even be bothered to stay here? Tell me Jackson, what could possibly be more important than this? Do you even care about your nephew?"

"I do." I shouted, louder than intended, my voice breaking. "Val, I care more than anything. I can't go into details right now, but something has happened that could affect all of us. I need to go make sure that it doesn't."

"Whatever." She replied, wiping her eyes once more.

"I love you, Val." I said, softly. She didn't reply.

I turned and began to leave the waiting room. Before I could make it all the way to the elevator, however, Jules called out behind me. I turned around to see her standing just inches from me. "Jackson…" She said. "You shouldn't be going anywhere or handling anything while you're like this. You're upset, you're not thinking straight."

Before I could stop myself, my hands were on either side of her warm, rosy face. Quickly, I pulled her in to a long, passionate kiss. I felt her heart beating fast as our chests pressed together. After several seconds, our lips finally parted. She stepped back, slowly, looking up at me with her warm brown eyes.

"Jackson…" She said. Her cheeks were bright red. Before I could reply, she slapped me across the face.

The doors to the lobby flung open, banging against the wall loudly. Through them burst a tall, brown haired teenage boy.

"Where's Austin?" He shouted. His face was red and swollen.

"Where is he?" He asked again.

"Who the hell are you?" Valerie said, standing to move towards him.

"I'm Austin's boyfriend." The young man replied. Nobody answered him. Valerie looked at him, intently, her eyes softening.

"I meant…" The boy stammered, clearly shocked that he had said the words out loud.

"Well?" Valerie said.

"I'm Graham. I go to school with Austin. We're friends. I don't know why I said that. I'm sorry, I'm just so worried…" His voice trailed off as he realized how foolish his lie sounded.

"Oh." Valerie said, clearly not believing a word he had said.

"Well, Austin can't have visitors right now, just family, that's all. Nobody else. When Austin wakes up, I'll let him know that you stopped by."

"But..." He began. He didn't finish the sentence. "Okay." He said, his voice cracking as he turned to leave.

"Get his number." I whispered, leaning in towards Jules.

Jules nodded in agreement and, with that, I turned and made my way into the stairwell. I flew down the ten flights of stairs in a haze, my brow wet with sweat by the time I reached the hospital lobby once more.

"Did you find your family, sweetie?" The nurse asked, sweetly, as I whizzed past her desk. "Yes! Thank you!" I shouted back at her, not turning around to make eye contact.

I pushed through the large revolving door, once more finding myself in the cold New York air. Stepping directly into the street, I hailed down the first cab that came whizzing by.

"I need to get to the Hotel Brynne as fast as possible." I said, sliding into the musty smelling cab and slamming the door behind me. The ten-minute ride felt hours long. When we finally pulled up in front of the hotel, I once again swiped my card and breathed a sigh of relief when an "Approved" message flashed across the screen. I made my way into the hotel's bright marble lobby.

"Hi." I said, abruptly, as I approached the desk.

"How can I help you?" Replied the bored, college-aged clerk, clearly annoyed that I had interrupted the episode of Orange is the New Black playing on his laptop.

"I'm looking for someone, I need to know their room number. Carlotta Winthrope is her name."

"I'm not allowed to give you that information, sir."

"It's a matter of life and death, I assure you." I replied, growing more annoyed by the second.

"I'm afraid…" He began.

"Look!" I shouted, cutting him off. "I'm sure you're not supposed to be sitting here watching Netflix while you work, either, yet here you are. Unless you want me to get in contact with a manager, I'd suggest you give me the fucking room number."

He looked at me for several seconds, shocked. Finally, he turned to the computer in front of him and began typing.

"What was that name again?"

"Carlotta Winthrope"

"Room 673"

"Thank you." I replied. "Have a blessed day!"

I walked several feet to the row of elevators located across from the main desk. Impatiently, I pressed the small, circular yellow button repeatedly until the metal doors finally slid open.

Reaching the 6th floor several moments later, I followed the sign that pointed me towards her room and found myself standing at the door just several seconds later. Immediately, I began banging rapidly on the door.

"Carlotta!" I shouted, my fists pounding the hard metal door. "Carlotta! Answer this goddamn door!"

No response.

"Carlotta!" I screamed, banging even harder. "Open the door!"

Finally, the sound of footsteps emerged from inside the room. There was a small "click" as she unlocked the door. She swung the door open, partially, looking at me with sleep still in her eyes. Her hair was messy, her face makeup free. She was wrapped in a silk robe, the hotel's initials emblazoned on the chest.

"Jackson, what the hell are you doing here? Do you know what time it is?"

I pushed past her, shoving the door open and moving into the room.

"What the FUCK, Carlotta?" I said, my voice shaking with anger.

"Jackson..." She started.

"How could you do this?"

"What are you talking about?" She said, moving towards me.

"That envelope you gave me. Did you take it and give it to a reporter?"

"No! What are you-" She started.

"You said you didn't know what was inside of it!"

"I didn't!" She shouted, her eyes wide with confusion. "Jackson what is all of this about?"

"You expect me to believe that somebody just dropped it off here for you, and you never looked inside? I never should have believed you, all you do is lie."

"Jackson, that's exactly what happened! I was getting ready for the funeral, and someone knocked on my door. I opened it and there was a man, dressed in all black. He handed me the envelope and said: "Please give this to Jackson". Then he turned around and walked away before I could even say anything!"

"You didn't think that was a little bit weird?"

"OF COURSE I did!" She said, exasperated. "I thought maybe it was from a crazy fan or something. Shit like that used to happen to you all the time."

"So this mysterious package appears on your doorstep and you never even think to open it? To question how anyone would even know that I know you?"

"I honestly just assumed it was some kind of crazy fan mail or something, Jackson. I don't know, I had bigger things on my mind that day."

"Like weaseling your way into a funeral, pretending to care about your brother so that you could get back into your daughter's life?" I snarled.

"What the hell is that supposed to mean?" She replied, her face covered in confusion and anger.

"Did you or did you not break into my house after that accident and give that envelope to the press?"

"What? Of course I didn't, Jackson! I don't even know where you live."

"You expect me to believe you couldn't find out? You're a master manipulator, Carlotta. You forget how many people I have watched you fuck over, myself included."

"Jackson, why would I even want to do that?"

"Who else would do it, Carlotta? Who else would have any reason to tell the world what was in that envelope?"

"Jackson, I don't KNOW what was in it! What is so important that you think I broke in to your home and stole it back from you?"

I didn't reply. I couldn't stop myself as the tears came.

"Jackson, what the hell is going on?" She said, her voice sincere. She moved towards me, reaching up to wipe my tears with the back of her hand.

"I wish I could explain it all to you…" I started, but I didn't finish the thought.

"Why can't you?" She asked.

"It's all too complicated right now."

"Let me be here for you."

She was standing just inches from me now. She lowered her hand from my face, grabbing my hand instead. Her touch was warm. I could feel her hot breath against my neck as she breathed in and out, intently. Our breathing slowly synchronized as I reached my hand up, brushing her long auburn hair from her face.

She reached her left hand to mine, covering it as it rested gently on her cheek. Our eyes locked for several long seconds. Finally, we moved in towards each other, our lips touching tenderly as my free hand pulled her closer to me.

We kissed, passionately, for several moments. Her touch sent a shiver down my spine. Heart racing, I began undoing the knot that held her silk robe together. It fell to the floor as she began undoing the buttons of my shirt.

We moved, slowly, towards the bed. I laid her down gently in front of me and stared at her for a long moment.

"You okay?" She asked.

"Yes" I said, smiling at her as I moved closer to her, kissing her neck.

When we finished making love, she rested her head gently on my chest.

"I've missed you, Jacky."

"I've missed you too." I said, stroking her head delicately.

Before long, she was fast asleep, snoring gently as she pressed up against me. I lay there, momentarily happy. Guilt crept up inside of me, consuming me with a dark, looming feeling. Gradually, I nodded off into a dream.

I was sitting on Valerie's couch, the glass of vodka still in my hand. I blinked the sleep out of my eyes, trying to remember where I was. My mind was hazy and my body hardly able to move. I could hear them, the voices coming from the den.

"Charles! Please keep your voice down!" Valerie pleaded.

"I'll talk as I please in my own goddamn house, thank you very much!" He shouted.

"Charles..." She began. But I couldn't make out exactly what she said.

The next sound I heard was the sound of his hand, slapping my sister across the face. Finally, I found the strength to move from the couch. Setting the glass of vodka down on the end table, I stumbled towards the den, trying my best not to fall.

"Get your fucking hands off of her." I said, shoving the door to the den open. Things went blurry as the room began to spin. I could hear myself talking. I could hear Valerie's voice talking to me, Charles shouting in the background.

The next thing I knew, my head was pressed against the cold tile of my sister's foyer. My eyes opened slowly, as I saw someone fleeing the house through the front door. In their hand was a large glass object, covered in blood. Someone I knew.

My mother.

Suddenly, I jolted awake, my body stiff and my brow soaked in a cold sweat.
Was this a dream, or a memory?

Carlotta lay motionless, breathing softly in her sleep, as I slid out of the bed and put my clothes on once more. Frantically, I exited the hotel room and made my way back to the lobby and out the front door.

Twenty minutes later I found myself banging on a different hotel door, the one belonging to my mother.

"MOTHER!" I shouted. "MOTHER! Open this door!"

The door flung open quickly, faster than I had expected.

"What is it?" She asked, her eyes wide with shock. "What's going on? Is it Austin?"

"This isn't about Austin." I said, moving past her into the room.

"Mother, where were you on the night of the 7th?" I asked, not looking at her.

"What?"

"The 7th. Where were you?"

"I was here! I wasn't feeling well that night. I was supposed to have a doctors appointment that day but cancelled it because I didn't feel well."

It was just then that I remembered that she was sick. Looking at her, really, for the first time, I realized how ill she looked. Her skin was gray and patchy, large bags formed under her eyes. She looked tired. "Oh..." I said.

I wasn't sure if I was ready for her to know that I knew she was sick.

"What is this about?" She asked, rather defensively.

"I..." I began. "I remember seeing you, at the house that night. The night Charles was killed. You were holding something, covered in blood." He eyes widened, her glance becoming cold.

"Don't be ridiculous." She said, sauntering past me and towards the large window, overlooking the city.

"I'm not going to call the police, I'm not even going to tell anyone about this, if I don't have to. I'm not going to send you to prison. That bastard deserved what he got."

"You shouldn't go around saying things like that." She said, her voice suddenly sincere.

"What does that mean?"

"I didn't kill Charles, Jackson." She said, turning to look at me once more.

"Then why..." I began.

"I was there that night, but I didn't kill him. He was already dead when I got there."

"He was?" I asked, my voice a thin whisper.

"Yes."

"Then why did you have...?"

"To destroy it."

"Where did you get it?"

"From somebody else, Jackson."

"Who?" I asked, my body going numb. Our eyes locked once more, as hers filled with tears.

"You."

CHAPTER TWELVE: Love is a Many Splendored Thing

"You're lying." I said. She didn't answer immediately, instead moving towards the couch to grab her large, designer purse. Reaching inside, she removed a pack of cigarettes, lighting one as she sat down. "I'm not."

"You did this." I said. My body had grown cold. I could feel my heart pounding against my chest.

"Jackson." She began, with a drag of her cigarette. "I didn't kill Charles."

"I..." I started." What are you saying?"

She looked at me, intently.

"Do you really want to know?"

"Yes."

"Sit down."

I moved, sitting down in the chair across from her. For several long seconds, neither of us spoke. She was staring out the window, my gaze locked tightly on her.

"Well?" I said, finally, breaking the silence.

"I'd known for a long time" She began. "About the abuse."

"How long?" I asked.

"Several years."

"Oh."

"There wasn't much of anything that I could do." She began, pausing once again to inhale from the cigarette. "I confronted her about it a while back, but she denied it all. Practically threw me out of the house."

"So you just let your daughter and your grandchildren stay there?"

"What was I supposed to do? Valerie and I aren't exactly close."

"Doesn't seem like you tried very hard."

"I never claimed to be winning any mother of the year awards." She turned, her eyes locking with mine. They were sharp, and dark. I had struck a nerve. "I'm trying." She said, her face softening.

I didn't reply.

"Life is short. There are things I needed to make right."

"Like what?"

"I had already been planning to pay you both a visit, when I heard about..." She stopped herself.

"Me trying to off myself?" I asked, coldly. She nodded, not looking at me.

"I came here to make things better..." She began.

"As always, you had a funny way of showing it."

"I don't know how to be that person."

"You have to try that hard to be nice to your own son?"

"That's a different conversation." She said, quietly.

"Fine." I said. "So what happened? You came back to town and decided to make things right by killing your daughter's husband?"

"I could tell that things were very bad as soon as I got here."

"So--"

"I knew she wouldn't open up to me, so I confronted him."

"I can't imagine that went well."

"It didn't." She said. Her cigarette was finished at this point. She pressed it down, firmly, several times in the ashtray located on the table next to her. She stared at it, intently, for several seconds before speaking again.

"I asked him to meet me at a restaurant, and to keep it between just the two of us. I knew Valerie wouldn't want us to meet, and that he'd have no problem lying to her."

"So he actually met you?"

"He did." She nodded, fumbling to light another cigarette. I wanted to tell her that I knew she was sick, beg her to stop smoking. "I told him that I knew he was hurting my daughter, and that I would be damned if I let it continue."

"And what did he say to that?"

"He laughed in my face. He didn't even deny it, the bastard. Just laughed and told me there was nothing that I could do - that I didn't scare him."

"If I know you at all, I know you didn't go there empty handed."

"Of course not." She said, chuckling slightly. "I laid out everything – almost everything- I had on him. Crime after crime that I knew he'd committed."

"How?"

"Being married to your father for so long had a few advantages, one of them being many, many connections." She said, smiling.

"Oh."

"He was a powerful man. He knew a lot of people, and I have a few connections of my own."

"So, what did he say?"

"He tried to blow it off." She paused, ashing her cigarette. "He told me that Valerie's name was tied up in the, which I had already figured out. knew he was bluffing. No way he was going to let himself go down, even if it meant taking her down with him. Not with an ego his size. I told him he needed to leave her.

"I'm assuming he didn't listen." I replied, my voice a low quiver once again.

"Actually, he did."

"What?"

"I told him he was to leave, to give her a generous settlement, and I told him that I would reimburse him for it. All he had to do was leave; it wouldn't even cost him a penny. She wouldn't argue it. She'd been talking to that divorce lawyer for months, trying to find a way out."

"Seems a little too good to be true."

"He agreed." She began. "But as we were about to leave, he grabbed my arm. Hard. He looked me in the eye and told me that if I said a word to anyone about what I knew, that he would kill her, and the children. She paused, inhaling sharply.

"Never in my life have I seen so much evil in someone."

"Oh my God." I whispered, my brow furrowing in shock.

"I knew that he had to be stopped."

"Killed?"

"Yes." She said, fiddling with the ashtray. She stood, slowly, moving towards the window once more. Grabbing a glass and the decanter of gin, she poured herself a drink, sipping it slowly. "I know…" She began, sipping once more. "That makes me no better than him."

"I'm just trying to process it all."

"I didn't have much to lose at that point. You'd be shocked what a mother would do for her children - even a terrible one."

"Even for me?" I asked, before I could stop myself.

"What?" She replied, turning to look at me, startled.

"What you'd do for your children…Does that include me?"

"Of course it does." She said. "I did it for you, too. I knew the secrets he had on you, Jackson. I knew everything."

"So what are you saying?" I asked, confused. "You went there to kill him – but you're saying I did it."

"I used my key to let myself into the front door." She began.

"You have a key to the house?" I asked.

"I had one made, yes."

So she would've had access to Madeleine's birth certificate, too. I didn't question her any further.

"When, I opened the door, I saw you lying there, on the floor. You were unconscious, your face smashed up against the tile. That's when I saw it, in your hand."

"You just took it?"

"The den was a mess. I went over to look, and that's when I saw him."

"Oh." I replied, dryly.

"I knew he was dead just looking at him."

"So why didn't you call the cops?"

"There's no crime without a murder weapon."

"Didn't you worry the cops might question you? That someone might have seen you?"

"Better me than you." She replied, her voice sincere. "I thought they'd see me on the security tapes, probably come to arrest me the next day."

"The detective told us there was no tape from that night. No record that the cameras were ever on. You didn't do that?"

"No." She replied.

Then who had? I didn't say anything for a long moment. Instead, I stood, making my way to stand near my mother. Slowly, I poured myself a drink. Raising the cup to my lips, I took a small sip. It burned slightly as the gin trickled down my throat.

"That doesn't mean I killed him."

"What?" She replied, surprised.

"You didn't see me do it, and I don't remember doing it."

"Jackson" She began. "I'm not going to tell anyone. If I wanted to, I already would've."

"No, mother." I said, quickly. "I'm not sure I did this."

Something caught my attention before she could reply. On the other side of the sitting area, an entertainment news program played across the large TV. The television was muted; I hadn't even noticed it on in the background. I noticed it now, my name printed across the screen.

"JACKSON ARRINGTON: BELOVED UNCLE OR DISGRACED FATHER?"

I scrambled to the other side of the room, fumbling for the remote on the table underneath the TV. I jammed my finger onto the volume button several times, until the anchor's voice was audible.

"Oft-troubled former child star turned hard-partier Jackson Arrington has found himself in what appears to be a paternity scandal!" The trying-to-be-serious, annoying grating male voice called out. "New reports tell us that the child his SISTER has been raising as her own is, in fact, Jackson's daughter. We've got an EXCLUSIVE copy of the alleged birth certificate on our website now. Stay tuned for more details."

"Holy shit." My mother's voice spoke out, softly, from behind me.

"I have to go." I said, turning towards the door. "This conversation isn't over!"

I slammed the hotel room door behind me, making my way back to the lobby as quickly as I could. Stepping off the elevator, I made a beeline for the front door, reaching for my cell phone.

She was standing across the lobby from me. Her long hair tucked behind her ears, wrapped in a long black coat. Her face was soaked with tears. I moved towards her, slowly.

"Carlotta..." I began, softly.

"You know, I followed you here." She said, cutting me off. "I woke up when you were leaving, and like some jealous, stupid little girl, I followed you here."

"I was here to see my mother."

"I don't care, Jackson." She said, her eyes filling with tears once more. "Here I sat, like an idiot, preparing to yell at you and make a scene and call some stupid girl an idiot for trusting you. Imagine my surprise, when I look up at the TV, and they're talking about you."

"Carlotta..."

"And they're saying that your sister is raising OUR daughter."

I didn't say anything.

"Is it true?" She asked, coldly.

"Carlotta..."

"Is it FUCKING true, Jackson?" She shouted.

"Yes"

"Oh my god." She said, bringing her hands up to cover her watery eyes. She let out a small whimper as she collapsed into the chair behind her.

"I didn't want you to find out like this." I said.

"You didn't want me to find out at ALL!" She screamed. Several people in the lobby were now staring at us. "I've been in town for how long now? You never told me. My daughter has been a few feet away from me, and you kept me from her!"

"It's more complicated than that, Carlotta."

"I gave her to you, I did. I know that. It made me feel like a better person. To think maybe you actually cared, that you would make sure she was taken care of, even when I couldn't."

"I did"

"You said you gave her away, to a good family."

"Yes-" I began.

"Really? My brother was an abusive piece of shit, Jackson."

"I didn't know that then."

"Madeleine…" She said, softly. "My daughter's name is Madeleine." I moved slowly towards her, sitting down next to her. I tried to take her hand, but she winced away from me.

"I can't believe this."

"I thought it was what would be best. I wanted to know where she was, that she was safe. I knew Valerie was a good mother."

"You wanted to stay in her life, without any of the responsibility." She said, coldly.
Her words stung me, deeply. Was I any better than my Aunt Charlene? Had I done exactly what I was so mad at her for doing to me?

"I didn't stay in her life…" I started, not sure if I was trying to convince her, or myself. "She didn't even hardly remember me when I showed up here. I wasn't in her life, she didn't know me or love me."

"You kept her close enough so that you could swing back into her life at any moment, which you did. You did exactly what was best for you."

"That's not true!" I started. My eyes were filling with tears. "I hardly…I hardly even paid her the attention she deserved once I moved in with Val. I was to ashamed, too worried about getting attached. It wasn't until Charles died that I started spending so much time with her. She needed me."

"She could've needed me!" Carlotta shouted. "You didn't give me the chance. You didn't give me the chance to know her, and now what am I supposed to do? Now that she's going to know the truth!"

"It would have been too complicated." I started.

"What would have, Jackson? I'm not suggesting that I would have told her the truth! I'm Charles' sister, for Christ's sake! I could have made a place for myself in her life as her aunt. I could have been content with that, the same way you were her uncle. You didn't allow me that."

"I didn't think of that, Carlotta. You have to understand, with your past..."

"MY past?!" She said, her voice a sharp whisper. "Your past is hardly any better than mine. Since you've shown up here, you've tried to kill yourself, and nearly your own nephew. But I'm the bad guy?" Her words stung. My eyes filled up with tears once again, as I finally noticed my cell phone vibrating in my pocket. I pulled it out, glancing down at the bright screen.

"Really?" She asked, incredulous. "You're going to check your phone right now?"

The screen was littered with texts and missed calls from Valerie.

"GET TO THE HOSPITAL. RIGHT NOW." The most recent one read.

"I've got to go." I said, standing and moving towards the door. "We'll talk soon, I promise."

"Fuck you, Jackson." She mumbled under her breath.

By the time I reached the hospital, my phone was ringing constantly. Texts and calls from people I hadn't spoken to in years, emails from my old agent, asking for a statement, requests from reporters, begging for interviews. I ignored them all.

I stepped off the elevator onto the 10th floor of the hospital and immediately saw Valerie, slumped in the same uncomfortable chair I had seen her in hours beforehand. I moved towards her, sitting down on the couch across from her. Our eyes locked for several long seconds.

"How did this happen?"

"I don't know."

"How did this fucking happen, Jackson?" She struck back, her voice clearly louder than she intended. The nurses at the nearby desk pretended not to hear her.

"Valerie, I really don't know."

"You're lying to me, Jackson." She said, her voice still cold. "Don't you fucking lie to me about this. I know you. I know you're lying, and I'm not going to listen to it.

You're going to tell me the goddamn truth. You owe me that."

I stared at her. Her face was tired and gray, her eyes were small, low and blood red from continuous crying. Her lip quivered as she tried her hardest not to break down once more.

"I received an envelope a while back."

"What kind of envelope?"

"An envelope that had Madeleine's original birth certificate in it. The one with my name on it."

"Who was it from?"

I hesitated.

"Jackson, who was it from?"

"Charles."

"What?" She asked, shocked. Her voice was dry, tight, as if the air had been sucked from her lungs.

"The envelope was from Charles."

"When did you get it?"

"The day of his funeral."

"I don't understand." She said, breaking our eye contact for the first time to stare down at her hands.

"It was as if he had arranged for it to get to me, if something were to happen to him."

"How did it get in someone else's hands? Who did you show it to?"

"Nobody! I swear to God, Valerie."

"Jackson, it didn't just hand itself over to the reporters. Somebody told them."

"When I got home earlier, I noticed it was missing from my desk. I tore my room apart looking for it, but it was too late."

Her eyes went dark for a moment. She stared at me, but I could feel her looking through me. Before she could speak again, a nurse entered the waiting room.

"Miss Sinclair?" The nurse said, softly.

"Yes?" Valerie said, her voice panicked.

"Your son is awake. You can see him now."

Valerie stood, immediately, and began following the nurse. I stood behind her, but before I could take a step, she swiveled towards me, pointing her long index finger at me.

"Where do you think you're going? You're not to be anywhere near my son." She turned, and was gone.

I sat down on the couch once more, lowering my head into my hands. The sobs came, uncontrollably, as my breathing became staggered and uneven. "Jackson?" Said the familiar voice.

Jules.

I looked up, and there she was, standing over me. Her hair was pulled back in a neat bun, her cheeks red as always. Her brow was furrowed in concern, her hand outstretched towards me.

"Jules." I said, taking her hand for a brief moment. "What are you doing here?"

"I'm about to start my morning shift. I came to check on everyone."

"Austin's awake, or so I heard."

"You haven't seen him?" She asked.

"Valerie won't let me."

"Oh." She said. "I'm sorry, Jackson. She'll come around." She sat down next to me, taking my hand once more and resting her head on my shoulder.

"Thank you for being here for me, Jules. I don't deserve it."

"Yes you do." She said, softly.

My mind flashed to the kiss we had shared just hours beforehand. Mere moments before I had slept with Carlotta.

"I really don't."

She didn't acknowledge my comment, instead sitting straight up and removing a piece of paper from her pocket. "Oh!" She exclaimed. "I almost forgot. I got that kid's name and number, like you asked."

She handed me the crumpled up piece of paper. I unfolded it. The name BILLY SANDERSON was scribbled across it, a ten-digit phone number sprawled underneath.

"Thank you." I said, smiling at her.

"This is probably the worst time to mention this, but, that kiss.."

"I'm so sorry." I said, cutting her off. "I shouldn't have done that."

"No!" She said, quickly. "I'm glad you did. I thought maybe I was crazy, these feelings I've been having for you. Maybe we don't know each other that well, but I want to be here for you."

She leaned in, wrapping her arms around me tightly. A twinge of guilt bubbled up inside of me. I didn't have much time to process this, however, as just seconds later; Valerie came charging back into the waiting room.

"I had a feeling you wouldn't have the common decency to leave." She snarled.

"I'll go." I said, standing.

"No." She replied, quickly. "He's asking for you." I didn't say a word. I made my way out of the waiting room, down the sterile white hallway, until I finally found Austin's room.

"Austin" I said, standing in the doorway, tears filling my eyes once again.

"Uncle Jackson." He said, smiling.

I moved towards him. As I reached the side of the bed, I grabbed his hand firmly, leaning down to kiss him on the forehead several times.

"I'm so sorry, Austin. I'm so glad you're okay."

"Me too." He replied, laughing.

"I met your friend." I said, smiling.

His face went blank.

"We don't have to talk about this, but I just wanted you to know that I love you, always."

He didn't reply for several seconds.

"When I met Billy, everything was different. I love him." He finally answered, whispering.

"That's great." I said, smiling at him.

"I'm not so sure anymore."

"Why?" I asked, concerned.

"I think he may have killed my father."

The needle pierced my skin, sliding deep into my neck. I felt as the liquid released from the syringe into my bloodstream. My whole body went warm as I fell to the ground. I lay there, paralyzed on the hospital room floor, my eyesight growing weaker as a blurred figure stepped over me.

The figure reached into their pocket, removing what looked like a washcloth. Pressing it to Austin's mouth, I heard his muffled screams in the distance as I lost consciousness.

CHAPTER THIRTEEN: General Hospital

I woke up, my eyes foggy with sleep. The bright, fluorescent lights above me became clearer and clearer, that sterile hospital smell filling my nose. Looking down, confused, I saw the IV in my arm, various wires surrounding and connected to me, machines beeping in the background.

"You're awake!"

I jumped. I hadn't seen Valerie propped in the ugly chair near the room's window.

"Valerie, what happened?"

"I was hoping you could tell me." She said, standing to move to my bedside.

I noticed, instantly, how tired she looked. Underneath her eyes were deep, heavy bags. Her eyes were puffy and bloodshot, filled with a sadness that, quite frankly, scared me. Her hair was unkempt, pulled back carelessly into a ponytail – something I had never seen before.

"What do you mean?" I asked, my voice still groggy and full of sleep.

Reaching the side of my bed, she grabbed my hand in hers, eyes filling with tears. "Do you know where Austin is? Did you see anything?" Suddenly, I remembered.

"What do you mean, do I know where Austin is?"

"Jackson, you have to tell me everything you remember."

"I went in to see Austin. We were talking, and then all of the sudden..." My voice trailed off as my mind filled with a thousand questions.

"All the sudden, what?" Valerie asked, her voice filled with panic.

"I don't know." I began. "I just remember feeling something, in my neck, and then I was on the floor, and I couldn't move. They went over to Austin. They were—" I stopped myself.

"They were what?!"

"They put a pillow over his face."

She sobbed, loudly, burying her head in her hands.

"Valerie, why did you ask me where he is? I don't understand." She looked up at me, her face streaked with tears.

"You had been in the room for about 10 minutes when a nurse came in to check on Austin. She found you, passed out on the ground. Austin, he was...he was just gone. And nobody saw him leave."

She paused. I didn't reply, didn't know what to say.

"Jackson...Who did this? Who would take my baby?"

Tears flooded my eyes. "Valerie…" I started. She cut me off.

"Are you okay?" She leaned over, kissing my forehead repeatedly. "I'm such a bad sister, I didn't even ask if you're okay."

"I'm fine, Val." I said. "Don't worry about me. We need to find Austin."

Before she could reply, the door to my room slid open and in slithered Detective Lewis, the same detective handling the investigation into Charles' murder.
"Mr. Arrington" He began. "I'm glad to see you're awake."

"Thank you." I replied, dryly. His presence still made me squirm. I had no reason to believe, necessarily, that he thought anyone in our family had killed Charles. Then again, I had no reason to believe that he didn't.

"Ms. Sinclair, could I have a moment alone with your brother?"

"I don't think that's a good—" She started.

"It's fine, Val." She leaned in, kissing me on the forehead one more time, before grabbing her purse from the chair behind her and moving towards the door.

"I'll be back in ten minutes to check on you." Val said, her voice filled with almost as much worry as her eyes. With that, she turned and exited the room, sliding the door closed behind her.

Detective Lewis moved the rolling stool from underneath the lab station towards my bedside, perching himself on it, just inches away from me. "So, I'm going to need a statement from you, Mr. Arrington." He said, his voice cool and emotionless.

"Since when do homicide detectives handle kidnappings?" I asked.

"Since the suspects are all the same." He replied, eyeing me intently. I didn't say a word. "I'm not the only one working on this case, if that's what you're asking."

Once more, I didn't reply.

"I'll need that statement, Mr. Arrington."

"I came into the room. I was talking to Austin, somebody must've come in behind me, but I didn't hear anything. Then I felt something, in my neck., like someone stuck me with something. I fell, I just remember lying on the floor and I couldn't move. Then this person just stepped right over me and..." My voice cracked, my eyes filling with tears.

"They grabbed a pillow and they put it over his face."

"So you're telling me that someone came in here, drugged you, killed your nephew, and then managed to dispose of the body without anybody noticing?"

My stomach lurched at his words. "I don't know that he's...No, he's not. He can't be. I just know what I saw. I can't think about that. You have to find him."

"I assure you, my team and I will do everything we can to locate him." His voice was still emotionless.

"You don't believe me."

"I didn't say that."

"Yes, but I can tell." I said, nearly shouting. My face was hot. "You don't believe me, but I'm telling you the truth."

"You've introduced a new person into this narrative. Before you woke up, we had no reason to believe there was a third party involved here."

"Then who did you think knocked me out?" I asked, confused.

"We didn't know that anyone did." He replied.

"What?"

"All we knew was that a teenage patient went missing, while someone with a long history of drug abuse and offenses was discovered lying unconscious in his room." His words sent a chill down my spine.

"Are you implying that I had something to do with this?" I shouted, incredulously.

"I'm not implying anything."

"Check the security footage! There are cameras in the hallway, right? They will show someone coming into, and leaving, this room."

"Already done, Mr. Arrington." He said, pausing to adjust himself in his seat. He looked at me, intently, for several seconds before continuing. "When I arrived at the hospital, you were still unconscious. In an attempt to, possibly, get a better grasp on what happened here, I asked the hospital security staff if I could view the surveillance tapes for the evening."

"And what did you find?"

"Unfortunately, there is no footage."

"What do you mean?"

"It appears there was a glitch in the system. A blackout. Nothing has been recorded by the hospital cameras in over five hours."

"Holy shit." I replied, my body growing tense. "You know what this means, right?"

"What does it mean, Mr. Arrington?"

"That somebody tampered with the cameras!" I shouted. "Whoever did this - It wasn't some random thing, this was planned! You have to see that!"

"We are looking into all possible explanations. I assure you."

"You're really going to waste your time blaming this on me, instead of looking for whoever really did this? Instead of looking for the person who took my nephew?"

"It is our utmost priority to bring your nephew home safely, if possible." He replied, coldly. "And to do so, we must explore all possible avenues."

"Why are you so intent on not believing me?"

"You seem to have pretty bad luck, Mr. Arrington. You were in the house when your brother in law was murdered, but you didn't hear a thing. You were in a car accident, but didn't see the driver of the other car, even as they fled the scene on foot. You were in the room when your nephew was, allegedly, abducted, yet you didn't see who did it, and neither did the hospital cameras. Seems like a lot of misfortune has fallen on you lately."

I stared at him, in shock, for several seconds.

"So now I'm a murderer, too? Is that what you're saying here?"

"Are you?" He replied, our eye contact unwavering.

"You told me weeks ago you had a lead in that case, some known criminal Charles was doing underhanded business with. What happened to that? You just throw it out the window because you don't like me?"

"I can't discuss that case with you, beyond what I've already informed you of."

"Of course you can't."

Before he could reply, the door to the room slid open once more. In entered Valerie, followed by a middle-aged nurse with a kind face.

"Alright, that's enough of that for tonight." The nurse said, making her way towards my bedside. "My patient needs rest."

"Fine." Detective Lewis said, gathering himself and standing from the stool. "When you're feeling better and out of the hospital, we will have to speak again."

I didn't reply. He moved towards the door, not stopping to look back at me as he exited the room.

"Don't worry about him, sweetie." The nurse said as she fidgeted with monitors next to my bed. "He's the worst. You need your rest."

"You know him?" I asked.

"For years now I have watched him come in here and attack patient after patient who were in no condition to be speaking to him. I have complained to everybody that I can think of about it, but nothing ever changes."

"Well, thank you." I said. "For getting him out of here."

"You're welcome, honey." She replied. "Now, I'm serious. You get some rest. The doctor will be in soon." She smiled at me as she left the room.

"What did he say to you?" Valerie asked.

"Nothing, really." I lied. "Just the usual, he asked some questions and stuff."

"Don't lie to me, Jackson."

"I'm not!" I lied, again. She moved towards me, her face drawn with worry.

"I know you aren't telling me something."

"You know how cops are, Val." I said. "They just want to "explore every option" and make you second guess yourself so they can tell if you're lying. It's just annoying, is all. Please, don't worry about it. He's going to find Austin, and if he doesn't, we will."

She smiled at me, tenderly, as she moved closer to my bed. Sitting down on the stool that Detective Lewis had left vacant, she reached out and grabbed my hand once more.

"I'm so sorry, Jackson."

"Sorry for what?" I asked, confused.

"I said some really awful things before. I was upset, but I shouldn't have taken it out on you."

"Valerie, it's okay. You were more than justified."

"I'm not happy that you took my son out in the middle of the night without my permission, but I know that you love him. I know you wouldn't deliberately put him in danger."

"He's a fantastic kid, Val. And he loves you very much."

"Jackson…" She began, her voice cracking. "What if he's…What if they…"

"Don't think like that, Val. He is fine. They will find him, and bring him home safe."

"I don't know what I'll do if they don't." She replied, with a sob. She buried her head in her hands, her crying now uncontrollable.

"It's all going to be okay, Val."

"I love you, Jackson." She said, looking up at me. Her voice was still thick with tears.

"I love you, too Val. Always."

"I'm glad you came home.. I'm sorry I didn't welcome you the way I should've."

"I dropped a kid off on your doorstep and then barely spoke to you for the better part of a decade. You had every right to be pissed off." I said, with a laugh. She chuckled for a moment, before growing somber once more.

"I wish I had taken better care of you, Jackson."

"What do you mean?" I said. "Valerie, you're the ONLY person who has ever taken care of me."

"I should've done more. I would give anything to be able to go back and take away all the pain you've felt. You've been through so much, and I know I could've done more."

"Valerie, you have taken care of me my whole life. I've taken and taken from you, and never gave anything in return. Yet, you have let me into your home and for the first time, made me feel like a part of something. You never could've given me anything more. I'm sorry."

She smiled at me as she wiped the tears from her eyes. Before either of us could speak again, the door to the room slid open once more.

"Hey, I just heard that you woke up, or I would've been down here sooner." Jules said.

"It's okay." I said, smiling at her.

"How are you doing?" She asked, moving closer to my bed.

"Well, I've been better. But I'm doing fine, all things considered."

"What exactly happened?" She asked. "It was all so scary. They found you in here and we had no idea what happened."

Before I could reply, yet another figure arrived in the doorway.

"Mother, you're back!" Valerie exclaimed, surprised. Our mother made her way into the room, walking right past Jules without so much as a glance.

"I'm sorry I wasn't here when you woke up." She said. "There was something I had to take care of. I got back as quickly as I could."

"I appreciate that." I replied, sincerely. She looked at me for a long moment, with a tenderness in her eyes that I'd never seen before. Jules interjected before she could reply.

"I'm really sorry, Jackson, but I have to go." She said. "I have to get up to the ER. I'll be back down to check on you when my shift ends." She turned and left before I could say goodbye. She seemed uneasy.

"So, what exactly happened?" Our mother asked, cutting the tension in the room with her words. Her voice had grown tense with worry and confusion. I explained things to her, just as I had done with Valerie and Detective Lewis.

"What did the police say?"

"That they'll look into it. There's no security footage, though. The cameras are down."

"Dear God." Our mother whispered.

"What were you two talking about?" Valerie asked, speaking for the first time in several moments.

"What?" I asked.

"You and Austin. Before it happened, what were you talking about? Did he say anything that seemed out of the ordinary?"

"No." I said, trying to think back on the conversation. "We were talking about Billy, actually."

"Billy?" Valerie asked, confused. "Who's Billy?"

"The kid who came in here before…" I paused, trying to find the right words. "The one who said he was Austin's boyfriend." Puzzled, Valerie exchanged a confused look with our mother.

"That boy said his name was Graham."

"No, no it was definitely Billy." I said. "Jules even got his name and number. I have it written down!"

"Jackson…" Our mother started. "The young man who came in to the lobby earlier, he introduced himself as Graham."

"No, I'm telling you, his name is Billy!" They didn't say anything back, exchanging another worried look.

"Where are my clothes?" I asked. "In my pants pocket, there is a piece of paper with his name and number written on it. It clearly says Billy."

Looking around for several seconds, our mother located my clothes, folded and placed on a shelf above the doctor's workstation on the other side of the room. Grabbing my pants, she lowered them from the shelf and reached into the pocket, pulling out the small white note that Jules had handed to me several hours beforehand. She read it aloud.

"Billy Sanderson." There was a long pause.

"I don't understand." Valerie began. "He introduced himself as Graham..."

"Are you sure you didn't hear him wrong?" I asked.

"How would I mistake "Billy" for "Graham"?" She asked. "Besides, mother heard it, too."

"I did." Our mother replied, confused.

"That doesn't make any sense to me." I said, pausing to think back.

Suddenly I remembered the young man bursting through the lobby doors. "I'm Graham", he had said.

"I think you're right, though.. I just don't understand why Austin said his name was Billy."

"So, what?" Valerie started. "Do you think there are two boyfriends?"

"Or maybe just one liar." Our mother muttered.

"How could there be two, when Jules went after him to get the information? Don't you think she would have noticed if she was talking to the wrong person?" I asked. At this, a look of questioning spread across our mother's face, yet she didn't say a word.

"That's true." Valerie said. "I don't understand."

"I'm sure there is a logical explanation." I replied. "When it's a more reasonable hour, I will call the number that kid gave to Jules, and I'll get to the bottom of that."

Our mother seemed unconvinced. "Do you think we should tell the police?"

"No." I replied, quickly.

Valerie looked at me, visibly surprised by my response. "Not yet." I said, calmly, thinking things over in my head. "This boy is just a kid, and if the police get involved, he's going to get nervous. If there is something he isn't telling us, we want to be the ones to get it out of him. Detective Lewis will scare him off."

"Are you sure?" Valerie started.

"He's right." Our mother said.

"Okay." Valerie replied, though she didn't seem convinced.

"Valerie, dear." Our mother said. "Could I have a moment alone with Jackson?" Valerie was visibly taken aback by the request.

"Oh, sure. Yeah. Okay. I'll be right outside, if you need me." She replied, her voice filled with pseudo-panic, as if she was nervous to be alone.

She stood, making her way through the doorway and into the hallway. Moving across the room, our mother slid the door shut and drew the curtains closed, preventing anyone from seeing into the room.

"What's going on?" I said. There was a nervous feeling rising in my gut.

"How long have you known this Jules person?"

"I met her right after I got to the city. She was my nurse when I was in the hospital before." Her stern expression did not change.

"And how did you become so...friendly?" She asked.

"She was my favorite nurse while I was in the hospital, she was very kind. When I left, she told me she recognized the pain I was going through, and told me that I should call her if I ever wanted to talk."

"You took her up on that?"

"Not at first." I said. "I ran into her at a bar, and she took care of me while I was pretty fucked up."

"You didn't think it was a bit odd that this nurse was so interested in getting involved with you?"

"It's deeper than that." I said, almost defensively. "She understood what I was going through. Her brother committed suicide."

"You think, as a nurse, you were the first patient she ever had that tried to kill themselves?"

"There's more to it than that!" I replied, my tone decidedly defensive now. "What are you getting at here?"

"I don't think she's who she says she is." She said, her face taut with concern.

"Some people are just nice." I replied.

"That may be true." She said softly. "But I don't think she is one of them."

"And what makes you say that?" I said, now growing angry.

"From the moment I first met her, I knew I had seen her before. I just couldn't remember where."

"Maybe you just knew someone that reminded you of her." I said, my tone changing as the doubt crept in.

"No." She replied, softly. "Earlier, she came in with her hair pulled back in a bun. That's when I knew who she was. That's why I had to leave."

"So what is it?" I replied. "What is it that you think she's done, that you think you know?"

"I told you that I knew for some time about the abuse your sister was dealing with, from Charles" She started. "Like I told you, Valerie wouldn't listen. She was afraid to leave him., but I wasn't afraid of him. I had him followed. I dug up everything on him that I could find, long before I was able to leverage him into agreeing to leave. And, of course, before his...unfortunate demise."

"So what does any of this have to do with Jules?" I asked, confused.

"Several months before all of this came to a head, I began to suspect that Charles was having an affair. He was having a lot of private meetings, and in locations that my private investigator couldn't get a picture of him in. So, I had no substantial proof. Eventually, however, as they always do, he slipped. My investigator found him having dinner with a woman at an assortment of very expensive hotel restaurants. Several times."

I didn't say anything. She opened her Birkin bag, removing a large manila envelope from inside.

"See for yourself." She said. "I didn't want to worry your sister with this, not now, but I think this speaks for itself."

She handed me the envelope. I fumbled to remove the contents from inside of it.
Inside the envelope were a series of photographs featuring Charles, across the table from a beautiful young woman, her hair pulled into a neat bun. In the last photograph, they both leaned in, sharing a kiss.

Jules.

The next few days flew by in a whirlwind. My mother and I did not speak of Jules again, and Valerie remained in the dark. I did my best to act normal around Jules, as I contemplated what to do about the situation.

While in the hospital, I was subjected to an obnoxious number of tests, as the doctors attempted to determine exactly what I had been injected with. When it finally came time for me to go home, I decided to first stop at the police station and get the sure-to-be reductive round of questioning over with as quickly as possible. Sure enough, Detective Lewis and I went round and round, rehashing the same exact things I had already told him in the hospital room. There was no advancement whatsoever in finding Austin, and I wasn't convinced that they were really looking that hard. I felt sick.

When I finished my round of questioning, I called for Valerie's driver to pick me up from the police station. Never in my life had I been so happy to see a town-car. When we finally arrived at the house, I made my way directly from the front door to the staircase.

"I'm home!" I shouted, already halfway up the stairs. "I'm going to take a shower! I'll be down in a bit." The truth was, I wasn't that interested in a shower. I just didn't want to talk anymore.

I entered my bedroom, closing and locking the door behind me. I immediately stripped myself of the days-old clothes that I had been forced to wear home from the hospital, and pulled myself into my favorite sweatshirt and gym shorts. Moving across the room, I sat down at the desk and flipped open the laptop that sat on top of it. Mindlessly, I clicked the email icon and waited as my inbox popped up, a flurry of unread messages begging for my attention.

One in particular caught my eye. The sender was unknown and the subject line simply read "AUSTIN".

My heart stopped. I clicked the message frantically, waiting for it to open. When it finally did, I saw that it was blank, save for a video attachment. A cold sweat forming on my brow, I clicked the video and waited as it loaded.

After several seconds, the grainy footage came into focus. It was a video of the hospital. Confused at first, it took several seconds for it to dawn on me – this was the lost security footage. By the time I figured this out, the clip had ended. I paused it, looking at the date and time stamp in the bottom right-hand corner.

It was labeled the date of Austin's disappearance, roughly 15 minutes after I had entered his room to talk to him. Frantically, I rewound the video to the beginning and let it play once more.

Fleeing the hospital in a frenzied rush was a woman, dressed in all black. Her head was wrapped in a floral scarf, and large sunglasses covered half of her face, but I recognized her. This was a woman I knew.

It was Aunt Charlene.

My birth mother.

CHAPTER FOURTEEN: The Bold & The Beautiful

I sat there for what felt like hours. Over and over again, I rewound the footage and watched as the woman I'd known as my Aunt Charlene crept out of the hospital. The hospital where I'd been drugged - knocked out so that somebody could kidnap my nephew. Was that somebody her?

Staring at the screen for several more moments, I eventually heard a soft knock on the door behind me.

"It's open." I said, absentmindedly. I heard the door open, slowly.

"Jackson..." My mother's voice was soft, taut with nervousness. I turned towards her, our eyes locking. I didn't say anything.

"How are you doing?" She asked. "You've been up here a long time."

"What are you doing here?" I asked, ignoring her question. She was clearly taken aback by my icy tone.

"Valerie is out looking for Austin. Talking to everyone he knows, basically. She's running herself ragged. I'm very worried about her.

"You didn't answer my question." I said, coldly.

"She wasn't sure when you'd be home and she wanted to make sure somebody was here when Madeleine gets dropped off from her friend's house."

She paused for a moment. "Jackson, did I do something? You seem upset."

"Why don't you skip the bullshit and tell me what your sister was doing at the hospital the night Austin was kidnapped?" A wave of shock spread across her face, her eyes flickering with confusion.

"What are you talking about?"

"Charlene was at the hospital the night Austin was kidnapped."

"What do you mean she was there? You saw her?" She asked, her voice almost a whisper.

"No. I didn't, but I have a surveillance tape showing her sneaking out of the hospital, and I know you had something to do with it."

"Jackson, I swear…" She began.

"Stop it, mother." I exclaimed, angrily, standing to move towards her. "You know, I'll admit, you almost had me fooled."

"What are you..." She started.

"I'm doing the talking, mother!" I shouted, cutting her off. "You come back into town, as nasty as ever. You say horrible, mean things to me, and then all of the sudden - You're nice. After all these years, you suddenly feel bad about the way you've treated me? How convenient it is that this about face happens just as I remember seeing you with a murder weapon in your hand. Just as your sister blows back into town, revealing herself to be, possibly, an even worse person than you are. How convenient that only THEN do you have remorse."

"Jackson, you're upset. You're not thinking clearly."

"Why did you come here? What are you two planning?" I asked her, my voice filled with a quiet rage.

"Nothing!" She cried, her eyes glossed with tears. "I don't know what you're talking about. I didn't even know Charlene was at the hospital that day. I have no clue what she was doing there, but I promise you I had nothing to do with it."

"I don't believe you." I said, turning towards the desk on the opposite side of the room once more. I did believe her, and it terrified me.

"Jackson..." She began, reaching out to place her hand on my shoulder. I shrugged away, my back still to her.

"I came to town to make amends with you."

"Then why were you so horrible to me when you got here?" I asked, unable to fight the lump rising in my throat. I turned, once more, and moved towards the bed, taking a seat on its edge.

She didn't reply right away. Instead, she moved towards the row of windows, overlooking the street below. She stood there for several long seconds, gazing through the slats of the blinds.

"That's the only way I know how to be, Jackson." She turned towards me, her eyes wet with tears once more. I didn't say a word.

"I've always had to fend for myself. There wasn't ever anybody on my side."

"That isn't an excuse, mother." I said, my eyes locked intently on my hands, wringing nervously in my lap.

"You're right. It's not." She said. "I'm sorry."

I didn't reply. After several seconds, she moved once more, taking a seat next to me on the bed. She grabbed my hands in hers.

"You'd been on my mind for a long time, Jackson. I've known for a long while now that I owed you an apology, an explanation. I was too much of a coward. I can admit that now. It's not an excuse, but it's the truth. When you've spent a lifetime trying to be as unfeeling as possible, it can be hard to wrestle with real emotions, when they do come."

"So what caused this revelation?"

She paused, wiping her wet eyes with her free hand.

"Time is of the essence. When I found out you were in hospital, I knew."

She paused once more, this time inhaling sharply. Our hands slipped apart as she reached for her purse, pulling out a packet of menthol cigarettes. Her hands trembled, slightly, as she clicked the lighter several times. Taking her first drag of the cigarette, I stood and moved towards the window where she had stood moments ago.

"I was afraid I'd run out of time." She said, finally breaking the silence.

"But you knew that I lived." I said, not looking at her.

"It wasn't necessarily your time that I was worried about, Jackson." She replied, her voice cracking slightly.

My body went cold. I didn't reply. I didn't know how.

"I knew you'd lived, and you have no idea how happy I was to find that out. It made me realize how short life is. The demons that you have, they started with me."

She paused.

"Mother..." I began.

"I'm sick, Jackson." She said, spitting the words out with a rushed vulnerability, as if she weren't sure they would stick.

"I know." I said, turning to look at her. A look of confusion lay across her face.

"Your doctor left a message for Valerie, and she told me." I said, sitting down next to her again. This time, I was the one to grab her hand.

"I'm so stupid." She chuckled, a tear escaping from her tightly clenched eyes.

"I think Valerie was surprised to get the call." I replied.

"Who else was I supposed to list?" She asked, with a sad chuckle.

She turned her head away from me, staring intently at nothing at all. I looked closely at her. She seemed frail, her hands slightly bonier than I remembered, her few wrinkles just a tad bit deeper. For the first time, I felt sorry for her.

"Mom…" I began, but she cut me off.

"I have nobody to blame for that but myself." She said, wiping her eyes once more. "I'm not looking to place blame. I'm not looking for pity." Her voice was fragile, yet lined with that sense of stubborn pride she'd always worked so hard to portray.

"I wish you would've told me sooner." I said, unsure of how to proceed.

"And put that burden on you?" She asked, incredulously. "On top of all the other shit you've been dealing with?" There was a long, lingering silence, as both of us struggled to find the right thing to say.

"I'm - I'm here for you." I said, taking her hand in mine again.

"Really?" She said, chuckling. "Just a minute ago, you thought I was the antichrist."

"You have to understand, all I have to go on is a lifetime of our relationship and, up until now, I didn't have much reason not to believe the worst."

"How sad is that?" She said, her voice quivering. She looked at me for the first time in several moments.

"It is sad, but we can't change that. What matters now is what happens going forward."

"So, you believe me?" She asked, her voice springing with hope. "I assure you Jackson, I don't know what she is up to and I have no part in whatever it is."

"I believe you, mom." I said.

Before I had a chance to realize what was happening, her arms were wrapped tightly around me. Her head resting lightly on my shoulders, we sat like this for a long moment. My mother was hugging me. For a brief second, I was a little boy again, and everything was okay.

Finally, she lifted her head from my shoulders. Standing, she adjusted the ends of her crisply ironed blouse and moved towards the computer, where the frozen image of Charlene stared back at her in grainy black and white. She looked back at me, though my eyes were still locked on the computer screen.

"We need to focus on finding Austin, and figuring out if my sister had anything to do with this. I want you to know…" She paused. "If my time runs out before we finish this conversation, I love you. And I'm sorry."

Before I could stop myself, the tears sprung from my eyes.

"I…I love you, too."

"Now." She began, turning once more towards the computer. "Where did you get this video?"

"Someone sent it to me, anonymously."

"There's no way to track it?"

"I don't know much about that stuff, but I'm willing to bet whoever sent it did everything they could to cover their tracks."

"Why do you say that?" She asked.

"When Detective Lewis questioned me at the hospital, I asked him specifically about the security tapes, and he said that they had been wiped out."

"Yes, of course. You did tell me that."

"Well, this footage clearly came from the hospital cameras, which means whoever sent it, must have had something to do with the blackout in the security system. They're not going to want to get caught. Especially because, seemingly, the blackout was orchestrated to assist in a kidnapping, and that's a pretty serious charge."

"Yes, but..." my mother began, trailing off to gather her thoughts. "Well, this clearly incriminates Charlene, or it's supposed to. Why would someone who was involved in all of this go out of their way to expose her? Wouldn't they be working together?"
I didn't reply right away, my mind working in overdrive.

"Unless whoever it is has some sort of remorse?" I said, meant as a statement, though spoken as a question. "Or they're trying to pin the entirety of the blame on Charlene to cover their own ass."

"Or they're framing her." My mother replied, a note of hopefulness in her voice making it clear that, despite their contempt for one other, she hoped her sister wasn't involved.

"I suppose that's a possibility, too." I replied, contemplatively.

"So what do we do now?" She asked. "Do we go to the police?"

"They need to see it, eventually. That's for sure."

"Eventually?"

"I'm not so sure that Detective Lewis isn't out to get me." I replied, a touch of fear in my tone.

"What do you mean?" She replied, alarmed.

"He made this comment at the hospital the other day, about how suspicious it was that Charles was murdered and Austin kidnapped all since I came to town. He didn't outright say it, but it was clear that he thinks that I'm involved somehow."

"Do you think he knows?"

"Knows what?" I asked, confused.

"Jackson..." My mother began.

"Mother." I said, cutting her off. "I know what you saw, but I'm telling you I don't think I killed Charles. I really don't."

"Then who did?"

"I don't know, but I have a feeling it's the same person that took Austin."

"Jackson, I know you don't want to hear this, but..." She paused, gathering her thoughts. "Have you thought anymore about the pictures that I showed you? Do you think your friend Jules could know anything about this?"

Her words hit me like a train. The truth was, those pictures had been burned into my memory from the moment that she had shown them to me. I didn't know how to handle it. Jules had texted me several times since then, and I had been all but avoiding her completely. I knew she knew that something was wrong, and I knew it was time for me to do something about it.

"Just because she knew Charles, doesn't mean she's a murderer, or that she kidnapped Austin."

"You're right. But it does mean that she hasn't been honest with you, and it COULD mean either of those things. Even if she's innocent, she may know something that she doesn't even realize, something that could help us."

"I will talk to her and Charlene, before we go to the police."

"If that's what you think is best." She said. "Do you know where Charlene is?"

"No." I replied, taken aback. "I assumed you would, at least know where she was staying."

She nodded her head no, her hands playing idly with the cigarette butt she had smothered in an ashtray several moments beforehand.

"I haven't seen her since that day at the hotel. I didn't even know she was still in New York until you showed me this."

"Great." I replied, my voice dripping in sarcasm. "Well, I'll find her." Before she could reply, a call rang out from downstairs.

"Mom? Jackson? Are you guys here?" Valerie's voice called out, echoing off of the marble laden foyer.

"Coming!" I replied, as my mother and I made our way out of the bedroom and down the large staircase.

"Any luck?" Our mother asked from behind me as we reached the foyer.

"Not exactly." She said, moving through the foyer and towards the living room.

Following her, we made our way into the living room. I sat down in the large chair near the fireplace; our mother perched on the crisp white couch. Valerie stood at the sidebar, pouring herself a drink.

"I talked to the leaders of both of the clubs he's been involved in this year." She said.

"And?" I asked.

"They said he hasn't been showing up to meetings hardly at all the past couple of months."

"Oh." Our mother replied.

"What kind of mother am I? That I wouldn't even know that?" Valerie began, her face growing red, her eyes filling with tears.

"Valerie, you cannot blame yourself, for any of this. " I replied.

"I mean, he wasn't coming home, either. That's the thing." She started, pausing to take a sip of her drink. "All the times he was supposed to be staying after school for a meeting or a group or anything like that, he wasn't here. And, apparently, he wasn't there, either. So where the hell was he?"

"That's a very good question."

"What kind of mother doesn't know where her own child is?"

"Valerie." I began, standing to move towards her. "Austin was going through a lot, obviously, and he was dealing with it all on his own. He wasn't sharing this stuff with anyone, and that isn't your fault. He knows how much you love him, I know that for a fact."

"Well maybe if I'd shown him a little bit more, he would've confided in me, and I would some clue about his life that could help me find him now."

"Do you think..." I started. "Do you think that Billy kid might know anything?"

Her face tensed up, ever so slightly.

"Maybe." She said.

"Maybe we should contact him."

"I've tried." She said, taking another large swig of her drink. "The phone number he gave your friend is disconnected, and there's nobody with that name enrolled at Austin's school. I don't have any idea where

Austin would've even met him, let alone where I'm supposed to find him."

Nobody spoke for several seconds.

"I just don't understand how any of this happened." Valerie cooed, breaking the silence. "Where did my innocent little boy go? How did I not know he was going through any of this? What mother doesn't know? Who would want to hurt him like this? What could he have gotten himself into that would lead to this, and how would I not know? How could I not notice?"

"Val, I'm not so sure Austin's kidnapping had anything to do with his own issues."

"What do you mean?" She asked, taken aback.

"Don't you think it's possible, that whoever took Austin, is the same person that killed Charles?"

A look of sheer panic spread across her face. "No, no that can't be."

"What do you mean?"

"If that's true, that means that whoever has Austin is capable of murder."

"I didn't mean to upset you." I started.

"No, no that doesn't make any sense. Whoever killed Charles was obviously trying to punish him for something. He's already dead, so what good would taking Austin do? No, no this has to be something else."

Was she trying to convince me, or herself? Suddenly, thoughts of that night flooded my mind. Charles' body on the ground, Valerie's demeanor, her lies about how much she'd had to drink. Could she have been the one that killed Charles? If so, that would mean she's right, and Austin's disappearance was unrelated. A million questions flooded my mind.

"Okay, well we'll get to the bottom of this." I started. "I have a few things I need to do and some people to see. It's about Austin, or you know I wouldn't leave."

"Oh, okay..." She replied, her voice making it clear that she didn't really want me to leave.

"Madeleine will be home from her friend's house any minute." I said. "Are you okay?"

"Yes, yes I'll be fine."

"Okay, I'm going to go. Mom will fill you in on everything we talked about while you were gone."

I turned, starting to make my way out of the living room. After several steps, I stopped myself, turning around to make my way back towards Valerie. Throwing my arms around her, tightly, I embraced her in a hug.

"I love you, Val." I whispered, softly.

"I love you, too."

And with that, I left.

I made my way out of the house and down the busy Manhattan street in front of me. The cold air slapped against my skin, leaving my cheeks stinging and red. It would have been much quicker to call a taxi, but my mind was so full of questions that I hardly noticed the thirty-plus minute walk to Jules apartment building, until it was over.

Making my way into the building, I moved quickly up the creaky steps until I reached the level at which her apartment is located. I moved down the hallway, stepping over a small puddle of water on the ground as I reached her door, located at the end of the hall. I began knocking, profusely.

Several seconds later, the door to the apartment swung open. There stood Jules, her hair messy and tucked behind her ears, her small frame covered in a tightly tied robe.

"Jackson!" She said, clearly shocked to see me. "What are you doing here? Come in!"
I moved past her, not saying a word.

"Jackson, what's going on?" She asked, closing the door behind her.

"You know what I liked about you?" I said, turning quickly to face her once more.

"What?" She said, visibly confused.

"You were, I thought, the first person that was straight with me." I started, as I began pacing, slightly, back and forth across the room. "You were the first person where there was no bullshit. There were no pretenses. I thought it was different."

My face was on fire, a lump rising in my throat. I was getting more upset than I had intended. My emotions were rising inside of me like a violent storm, and I knew I needed to calm myself down.

"Jackson, what are you talking about?"

"Maybe I'm an idiot, Jules. Maybe I am. Maybe I was just in a really shitty place and needed someone to count on, and you were there. So I made you out to be something you weren't. I believed everything you said."

"What are you talking about, Jackson? What is going on?" There were tears in her eyes.

"You knew who I was. You recognized my name. You were upfront about that." I said.

"Yes."
"What you didn't tell me was that you also knew someone else in my life, someone I was stupid enough to talk to you about."

Her eyes grew wide.

"What are you talking about?"

"What does the name Charles Sinclair really mean to you, Jules?" I asked, coldly.
Her face went white. She stood, silently, for several seconds. Our eyes were locked on one another.

"It's not what you think." She began.

I let out a cynical laugh. "Oh my god, I cannot even believe you just said that. Has there ever been an instance where someone started a story that way and it WASN'T exactly what the person thought?"

"Yes, Jackson. I swear to you."

"Why wouldn't you have told me, then, Jules? I went on and on to you about the way he treated my sister, about his death, about his CHILDREN, for god's sake. And you sat there and acted like you were some stranger, but you knew him! You were probably fucking him, weren't you?"

"You've got it all wrong. I didn't tell you that I knew Charles, because it's very complicated."

"Oh, please. Don't tell me you were in LOVE with that monster?"

"Absolutely not." She said, her voice stern and honest.

"Then what is it?" I shouted back at her.

"I hated that bastard just as much as you did, I promise you that!" She shouted, her voice straining and cracking as tears fell down her pink cheeks.

"Why is that?" I asked, confused, as millions of emotions collided inside of my mind.

"He is the reason that my brother killed himself."

CHAPTER FIFTEEN: Dark Shadows

I felt my stomach lurch. My face, hot with anger just seconds beforehand, was now cold, my mouth dry, as the lump in my throat grew.

"What are you talking about?" I asked, my voice barely a whisper. She didn't reply right away. Instead, she moved past me, towards a small table that sat next to a large, bay window. She reached down, picking up the small wooden frame that held the picture of her brother.

"Everything I told you about my brother was true." She said, breaking the silence with her soft words.

"How can I believe that?" I asked.

"I would never lie about him." She snapped, slamming the picture down and turning to face me once more. Her face was angry, but her eyes were sad. I knew she was telling the truth.

"Okay." I began. "But everything else was clearly a lie."

"That's not true."

"You met me. You knew who I was. I shared things with you, intimate things about my family, about Charles, specifically. And all this time, you knew exactly who he was. You knew HIM. Yet you never said a word."

"Because I didn't realize, Jackson..." She started.

"Realize what?"

"I recognized you in the hospital, yes. For the exact reason that I told you - because of my brother. It wasn't until much later, when you mentioned Charles, and you told me about him, that I put the pieces together. I should have been honest, I know that. Then, he was killed, and everything got so complicated, and I really started to like you Jackson. So I didn't say anything."

She looked directly at me, but I averted my eyes, instead focusing my stare on the picture of her brother, now lying inside of a broken frame.

"Did you kill him?" I asked, my voice cool and unwavering.

"What?" She gasped, incredulously. "No! Of course not! How could you ask me that?"

"Apparently I don't know anything about you, Jules. Why wouldn't I ask?"

"You DO know me, Jackson. You do! I know I wasn't honest about this, but it doesn't change what I've told you. It doesn't change how I feel about you, or who I am as a person."

I ignored her statement; instead moving several feet across the room to sit on the worn, red couch perched under the window. I felt the room begin to spin as my breathing became more and more sharp.

"What did you mean before?" I started, pausing to wipe the newly formed sweat from my brow "About Charles, and your brother?"

"Jackson, are you okay?" She asked, moving towards me.

"Answer the question!" I snapped.

She paused for a moment before speaking again. "Charles is –" She started. "Charles *was,* the reason my brother took his life."

"What do you mean? I don't understand."

She stood for a second without replying, before turning and moving towards me. She paced for a second before sitting in the wingback armchair across from me.

"I told you that my brother struggled a lot with depression." She said, not making eye contact with me.

"Yes." I replied.

"He was always so hard on himself, always putting himself down. He loved computers, and he was incredible with them. I mean, he could do anything."

"What does that have to do with Charles?"

"He used to go to these events, these like, computer programming events. I don't really know what they were for, but when he went to them, he was genuinely happy. That was so rare for him, so my parents never minded paying for him to go."

She paused. Her eyes darted once more to the photo of him on the end table.

"About a year before he died, he came up here for a convention. He was so excited, apparently it was some big deal, and he was staying with me. We were having a wonderful time, but that was also when he met Charles."

"I didn't think Charles was into computers." I said, confusedly.

"He wasn't." She replied. "That's how they bonded." She paused for a moment, but I didn't speak. Eventually she looked up at me, before continuing.

"They were both at the hotel bar. Charles was having some issue or another with his computer I guess."

"And your brother helped him." I interjected. I instantly felt bad for speaking, as if I had interrupted her. She nodded.

"Daniel came home that night talking all about it. I had never seen him so excited."

"What exactly happened?" I asked.

"I guess Daniel could tell that Charles was having trouble, so he went up to him. Charles was pretty rude at first."

"No surprise there."

"Well, eventually, he must have realized that Daniel could help him with whatever the issue was, so he let him, and he was really impressed with what he saw."

"Charles was always appreciative of people that could do things for him."

She didn't reply. A twinge of guilt rose up inside of me. "I'm sorry. That was insensitive."

"No." She shook her head. "You're right."

"So what happened after that?"

"Charles took him under his wing. Offered him a job. They were practically attached at the hip. Within a couple of months, Daniel was going everywhere that Charles went."

"He was happy?"

"Yes." She said, pausing as tears fell from her eyes for the first time. "I'd never seen him so happy. Ever. It was like he was a whole different person. From a selfish standpoint, I was happy. He was living here in New York. I was seeing him all the time. I didn't have to worry about him, because I knew he was right around the corner if he needed me, and I knew he was happy."

"That isn't selfish, Jules. You clearly loved him very much."

"It was selfish." She said. "I was blind to what was really going on. I should have asked more questions. I should have seen the signs."

"Maybe there weren't any."

"No, there were. When things would get stressful at work, he would have panic attacks. He was always so worried that he was going to get fired. I thought it was just his anxiety creeping back in, but I should have realized. I assured him. I told him Charles was his friend. I encouraged him to stay in that environment. I could have gotten him out."

"You didn't know." She didn't reply. She raised her hands to cover her face, letting out a wavering sigh.

"So what happened? What did Charles do to Daniel to make him..." My voice trailed off.

"There was some legal trouble. I still don't know the extent of it, but the FBI was looking into some of Charles' business ventures."

"Valerie told me that, as well."

"And, of course, Charles wasn't going to go down for it. From what I understand, he always had a fall man ready to go."

"Jules, what did Charles do?" She stood from the chair and turned, facing towards the window once more.

"Everything was in Daniel's name. Documents, emails, all kinds of things that made it look like Daniel was behind it all. Some of it might've been fake, some of it he might've tricked Daniel into signing or doing, I'm not completely sure. But the FBI showed up at Daniel's door and raided the place. From there on out it became clear that he was going to take the fall."

"And so he..." I stopped myself.

"He asked our parents to come here." She said, turning to face me again. "He sat us all down for dinner and explained to them what was happening. He seemed calm. At the time I thought he was just trying to stay sane, now I realize he had already decided to..." She didn't finish the sentence.

"I'm so sorry, Jules."

"He told us he loved us. He told us that everything would be okay. And then he went home, and he killed himself."

Neither of us spoke for a long moment. Jules looked intently at the ground in front of her, while I looked directly at her. There was sadness in her eyes. A sadness I recognized all too well, a feeling of failure. "I can't even imagine what that must have been like for you, for your parents."

"You're lucky. You didn't die. You tried to die and you didn't. You got a second chance."

Her words stung. My face grew hot. She was right. "You're right."

She moved across the room and sat down next to me, propped against the opposite arm of the couch, facing me.

"After Daniel died, I made it my mission to destroy Charles. I researched him, his businesses, his past, even his family. I followed him, figured out where his favorite restaurants were, when he went there, who he was with. Then one day I made it happen. I introduced myself to him. I flirted, and just like that, I was in. I wasn't going to stop until I had cleared my brother's name."

"Did you find anything out? Anything that could clear Daniel?"

"No. But I didn't have much of a chance. We had dinner a few times, but conversation was very casual, flirtatious. Eventually he started talking to me more, opening up a little bit, and I thought I might be getting somewhere. But then..."

"He was murdered."

She nodded.

"Wow. That's a lot to take in."

"Imagine living it." She replied.

I looked at her, our eyes locking for a moment. I reached my hand out towards her, grabbing her hand from out of her lap.

"I am so sorry for the way I came over here, Jules. I never should have said, or even assumed, those things."

"You're right. You shouldn't have." She said. "But I forgive you. I care about you."

She squeezed my hand before letting it go and smiling at me. "What's going on with Austin?"

"Not a goddamn thing." I said, frustrated. "Valerie is killing herself over this, obviously, and I don't think the police are doing a damn thing to help. I think I might have an idea of who's involved."

"Who?" She asked, surprised.

"My Aunt Charlene."

"Excuse me?"

"Somebody anonymously sent me security footage from the night Austin was kidnapped and there, clear as day, was my Aunt Charlene leaving the hospital right after Austin went missing."

"Holy shit. Have you talked to her?"

"No. That's my next step."

Just then, I felt my phone vibrate in my pocket. I pulled it out to see a text from my mother:

"Charlene is staying at the Grand Pier Hotel. Thought you'd like to know."
I smiled to myself.

"What is it?" Jules asked.

"I should have known my mother would figure it out."

"What?"

"She found Charlene. I have to go talk to her."

"Oh. Yes, of course. Go. But please call me later, and let me know what happens."

"I will, of course."

We both stood from the sofa. I leaned in, wrapping my arms around Jules waist, holding her tight in the hug.

"Thank you, Jules. For everything."

I left the apartment, Jules shutting the door softly behind me. I lingered for a minute, an uneasy feeling in my stomach. I heard Jules fumbling around inside of the apartment. Suddenly, she spoke, on the phone, perhaps? I leaned in to the door, trying to decipher her conversation.

The only word I could make out was "Austin".

The car ride to my aunt's hotel was a complete blur. One moment I was leaving Jules' apartment, and the next I was at the front desk of the Grand Pier, asking for my aunt's room number. After some arguing with the woman at the front desk, I finally got the room number and made my way to the eighth floor.

As I approached the door, a nervous feeling rose in my stomach. Could she really be capable of this? I raised my hand and knocked on the door lightly several times. A few seconds later, I heard her shoes against the tile floor as she moved closer to the door. Finally, she swung it open.

"Jackson!" She said, clearly surprised to see me. "What are you doing here?"

"Can I come in?"

"Of course." She said, moving to the side. I moved past her and into the large hotel room.

"We need to talk about Austin."

She turned to look at me, closing the door behind her. Her face wore a look of confusion and nervousness.

"What about him?"

"Let's skip the bullshit, Charlene. I know you were at the hospital."

"Oh." She said.

Before continuing, she moved past me towards the opposite side of the room. As she reached the mini-bar, she grabbed an already opened bottle of vodka from the shelf above the refrigerator. As she poured herself a glass, she turned towards me and spoke once more.

"Would you like a drink?"

"I said I wanted to skip the bullshit."

"I'm not sure what you want me to say." She replied, raising the glass to her lips, before pouring a second glass and handing it to me. I gulped it down, wincing.

"I want you to tell me what the fuck you were doing at the hospital."

"I was there to check on Austin." She cooed.

"You don't even know him."

"He's my family, Jackson."

"You don't give a fuck about your family."

"That's not true." She replied. "You may not believe it, but I care very much for my family."

"That's neither here nor there. I want to know what you were doing at the hospital."

"I've just told you. I was checking on Austin. I heard about the accident and..."

"How?" I asked, cutting her off.

"It's a matter of public record, Jackson. I have access to the news, you know."

"Are you having us followed?"

"No." She said, taking another sip of her drink. "But, let's just say, when something like that happens, I am informed."

Her words sent a chill down my spine. My lack of a reply must have struck a chord with her, as she moved closer to me, before speaking once more.

"I know you may never believe this, but I care very much about you – and everyone else in the family, for that matter. That's why I was there – to see how Austin was doing, with my own eyes. I didn't even realize that anyone had seen me."

I ignored her obvious bait. I wouldn't tell her how I knew she was at the hospital – not this easily. As far as she was concerned, I saw her with my own eyes, and it needed to stay that way.

"So why did you hide? You clearly didn't want to be seen."

"I didn't want to cause any trouble. I knew I wouldn't be welcome there, and the last thing that any of you needed was more drama. Especially on a day like that."

"What exactly did you see while you were there? Did you speak to Austin?"

"No." She said, nodding her head. Her gold bracelet, hanging loosely around her small wrist, clinked several times against the glass in her hand. "When I arrived, you were in the room speaking with him. I saw that he was okay, that you and Valerie were okay. That was all I wanted."

"You'll have to forgive me for being a bit skeptical of your motives."

"I don't blame you one bit." She replied, her voice quivering slightly. "You have every reason to hate me."

I didn't reply.

"What exactly is it that you think I've done, Jackson?" She continued. "Why do you think I was at the hospital that night?"

"As I'm sure you're aware, Austin has been kidnapped."

"Yes, I did hear that." She said, softly. "I can't even imagine what Valerie is going through."

"Why?" I shot back. "Because you never lost a child that you gave a damn about?"
Her face went blank. She looked down at the now empty cup in her hands.

"What do you want from me, Jackson?"

"I want you to say something that will convince me you didn't have something to do with Austin's kidnapping."

"I wish you had a better opinion of me, that you wouldn't think I'm capable of something like that."

"Well, I don't."

She moved towards me, reaching up to stroke my cheek, quickly, with the back of her hand.

"Oh, Jackson." She said. Her eyes had tears in them. "I promise you that I had nothing to do with Austin being kidnapped."

"You know, all my life I idolized you, longed to have you back in my life. As it turns out, you're everything that I thought I hated in my mother."

"So that makes me a kidnapper?"

"It makes you a liar." She didn't respond. I turned, moving away from her and back towards the door to the room. As I reached for the handle, I turned to speak to her once more.

"I love Austin." I said, my voice soft but harsh. "And if I find out that you had anything to do with this, I will stop at nothing to make sure that you pay."

Before I knew it, I was pulling up to the house. I made my way, halfheartedly, towards the front door. My body was sore, my eyes barely open from lack of rest. My mind cried out for sleep. All I could think of was getting into my bed and sleeping for as long as humanly possible. Maybe when I wake up, everything will have fixed itself.

I fumbled with my keys until finding the right one and inserting it in the lock. I pushed the door open and made my way into the foyer, pulling the heavy door closed behind me. I turned, clicking the lock into place, and moved towards the stairs. Just as I was about to begin the ascent into my room, I heard voices from Charles' office.

Confused, I moved across the foyer and towards the doors to the office. As I got closer, the voices became increasingly distinguishable. Valerie was in Charles' office, and she was speaking to another woman, whose voice I recognized, a woman that I knew all too well.

Carlotta.

I inched closer towards the office, leaning my ear towards the door to listen.

"Your fatal error here, Valerie, is assuming you have all of the power." Carlotta growled, clearly angered.

"Don't threaten me." Val replied, a steely fire arising in her voice. "And don't fool yourself. You have no power here. Or anywhere for that matter."

"I want access to my daughter, Valerie." Carlotta said, icily.

"She is MY daughter. You relinquished any right you had to her."

"I'm not asking to be her mother, but I WILL be in her life. You'd better be sure of that."

"What did I just say about threatening me? Did you forget that I have the power to destroy what's left of your life?"

"You think you do." She replied, chuckling slightly. "But you're sadly mistaken."

"I am financially supporting you. Don't fuck with me. I have information on you that I'm sure the police would love."

"Yes, but you're not going to use it." Carlotta replied.

"What makes you so sure of that?" Valerie asked.

"Let's just say you do go to the police, Valerie." She replied, menacingly. "Then I would have to have a little conversation with them myself. About you."

"I'm not scared of you." Valerie said.

"You should be." Carlotta replied. "Because I'm sure the police would love to hear all about how you paid me to take down my brother, with any means necessary."

CHAPTER SIXTEEN: Ryan's Hope

"What are you talking about?" I asked, frozen, from the entrance to the den. Carlotta turned to look at me, a look of shock across her face. Suddenly, Valerie pushed past her, making her way out of the den and towards me. "Don't believe a word she says." She replied, reaching out to take my hand. I pulled away from her.

"What is she talking about, Valerie?" I asked, my gaze still locked intently on Carlotta.

"You only heard a very small part of the conversation." Valerie replied.

"Seemingly the most important one." I shot back.

"It's a lot more complicated than that." She said.

"Just tell him the truth, Valerie." Carlotta said, speaking for the first time. "At this point, he has the right to know."

"The right to know what?"

"I did ask Carlotta to come here, but I never intended for anyone to die." Valerie replied, her voice earnest.

"At the funeral you acted like you'd never met before, you introduced her as Jacqueline." I said.

"We weren't exactly looking to broadcast our relationship." Carlotta replied.

"So I'm assuming you didn't come to New York the day of the funeral." I asked.

"No." Carlotta replied. She moved towards me for the first time. "I had been in town for almost a year at that point."

"A year?" I shouted. "What the fuck?" Before either of them could reply, I made my way into the living room and poured myself a drink. I sipped it, not turning back to look at them.

"I was trying to get away from Charles, I thought Carlotta might be able to help me." Valerie said, entering the living room with Carlotta in tow. "Nothing was supposed to happen the way that it did."

"What does that even mean?" I asked, locking eyes with Valerie. "How does Carlotta have anything to do with you getting away from Charles?"

"I had information about Charles, information that Valerie didn't have." Carlotta said, interjecting. "Information that could help put him away."

"I don't understand. I thought that you didn't even have a relationship with Charles." I said.

"I haven't been completely honest with you about that." She inched closer to me. "Or anything else, for that matter." I replied.

"I knew about Madeleine." She said, averting her eyes from mine.

"What do you mean?" I asked, feeling my throat tighten. Valerie, growing visibly upset, seated herself on the sofa, her eyes darting between us.

"Charles was involved in a lot of underhanded things." Carlotta began. "That went far beyond shady business dealings."

"What does that even mean?" I asked, refilling my drink.

"Charles' owned a vending and distribution company that provided food to several prisons throughout the country, namely in California." She began. "They were using the food deliveries to smuggle drugs."

"So Charles was what, running a prison drug ring?"

"His company was getting the drugs into the prisons, and he was profiting from it."

"What does that have to do with you?"

"They were looking to expand their territory, and I had connections that were valuable to him."

"How so?"

"You know as well as anyone, Jackson, that I have been involved in some less than stellar shit, most of which pertained to drugs." She paused, clearing her throat. "There was a very powerful man named Joseph Spencer, who I knew very well during my time in California. He was arrested in a drug sting a few years back."

"I still don't understand how that makes you any help." I said, confused.

"Charles had no connections at that prison, but he was looking to change that once he secured a vending contract with them. He wanted Joe's help distributing drugs, and he needed access to his connections to do so."

"And you gave him that?" I asked. "You just handed him information so that he could get prisoners hooked on drugs for profit?"

"Charles came to me." She said, wiping away tears. "I was in a lot of trouble, and I owed a lot of people money. He said he could make all of that go away if I helped him."

"Cover your own ass at the expense of everyone else. Typical." I shot back.

"I didn't say I was proud of what I did." She replied. "I needed help, and Charles could give it to me."

"Self serving runs in her blood, after all." Valerie said, speaking for the first time in several moments.

"The information that I gave him came through, and he was thrilled. That's when he told me about Madeleine. I don't know how he knew, but I imagine for someone like Charles, information like that would be easy to come by."

"So, what?" I began. "He let you see her?"

"No." She replied. She paused, blinking back tears. "He told me that if I continued to help him, as a point of communication, he would let me know my daughter."

"I'm assuming that promise never came to be." I responded.

"Charles never kept his word about anything." Valerie replied, coolly.

"When I had given him everything I had to give, he told me it was time to move to New York. I thought that I was coming here to establish a relationship with my daughter."

"How'd that work out for you?"

"He set me up in an apartment, with money, with everything I could have asked for. And then he fucked me over."

"How so?" I asked, confusion growing in my voice.

"He set me up on bogus drug charges, and had me arrested."

"Holy shit."

"It wasn't anything all that serious, but I spent six months in jail and another six on probation. Actually, that just ended recently."

"Charles never had any intention of letting her anywhere near Madeleine. Not because he was a worried father, but because he was a piece of shit who was willing to walk all over anyone and everyone to get what he wanted." Valerie said, standing from the couch and pouring herself a drink.

"So you two teamed up as what, some kind of revenge?" I asked. "The scorned wife and the jilted sister come together to kill the man they both hate? Sounds like a Lifetime movie."

"Nobody was supposed to die, Jackson. I told you that." Valerie replied.

"Forgive me, it's hard to decipher which things you've told me are lies, and which are true."

"I don't have a reason to lie to you about any of this, Jackson." Valerie said.

"Yet you've lied to me about everything."

"I have protected you!" She shouted, slamming her glass on to the table. "Just like I have done your entire fucking life!"

"Save it, Valerie." I replied, choking back tears. "This isn't about protecting me."

"I found out that Charles had been in contact with Carlotta, and I knew that he was responsible for sending her to jail." Valerie began. "I contacted her because I knew she had information that could be valuable to me, and that she probably hated Charles as much as I did."

"All we wanted to do was send him to jail, without taking Valerie with him."

"Why would you give a fuck about what happened to Valerie?"

"Selfish motive, like I said." Valerie replied.

"That's not true." Carlotta rebutted. "Yes, I wanted a relationship with Madeleine, but Valerie is her mother, and of course I care what happens to her."

"None of it matters anyway, because Charles is dead now." Said Valerie, icily.

"And I'm supposed to believe neither one of you killed him?" I asked.

"You can believe whatever you want, but that is the truth." Valerie said, her voice almost a whisper.

"I just don't understand why you never have enough respect for me to treat me like an adult." I said, to Valerie.
"That isn't true." Valerie replied.

"Bullshit." I shouted back. "You knew Tabitha wasn't my mother, you didn't tell me. You knew all about Carlotta, and you flat out lied to me about it. You don't trust me. You don't think I can handle anything."

"Because you fall apart, Jackson!" She cried. "Harder than anyone I've ever known. You crumble, and you self destruct, and I have spent your entire life trying to save you from that."

"By treating me like a child? How does that protect me in this situation?"

"I have no idea who killed Charles, but someone is out there who hated him even more than any of us did. Someone dangerous. I wanted to protect you from that."

"How do you know it wasn't me?"

The room went silent. Valerie and Carlotta looked at each other, and then me. "Was it?" Carlotta asked.

"I don't fucking know!" I said, the tears coming now. "I have been replaying that night in my mind, incessantly, afraid that I might've done this, or that someone I love did."

"I don't think you are capable of killing anyone." Valerie said, softly.

"You don't think I'm capable of anything!"

"That is not true!" She shouted, her voice cracking.

"Some days, getting out of bed feels impossible." I said. "Then, in the blink of an eye, being in bed makes it impossible to breathe. My mind is at constant war with itself, destroying me from the inside out. And now someone has been murdered, but the only thing I feel is worry. Worry that I might've had something to do with it."

"Oh, Jackson." Valerie whispered.

"Our mother was here that night." I said.

"What?"

"She came to confront Charles, and when she got here I was passed out on the fucking floor with the murder weapon in my hand."

"What are you talking about?" Carlotta said, her face furrowed in horror.

"I remembered something, a while back. I was fucked up beyond belief, but I remember hearing you and Charles arguing in the den. I tried to stop it, and the next thing I knew I was on the ground, passed out."

"Fuck." Valerie said, taking her seat on the couch once more.

"So maybe you did kill Charles." Carlotta said, a look of surprise on her face, as if she hadn't meant to say it out loud.

"No, there's no way." Valerie replied.

"You're the only other person who was there Valerie, only you would know." I said, avoiding eye contact.

"You came in and broke up the fight, and then I went upstairs. I was drunk." She said, admitting this for the first time. "Charles kicked us out of the den, and slammed the doors behind us. I went upstairs, but I could've sworn you came with me."

"Except I obviously didn't."

"Jackson, you were absolutely trashed. You could barely stand up, there's no way you could've overpowered Charles."

"Then who?"

"What about our mother? Detective Lewis told me that the wound appeared to have been inflicted by someone shorter, smaller than Charles."

"If I couldn't overpower Charles, you think a terminally ill woman in her 60's could? Was the murderer someone small, or someone blackout drunk operating with half his strength?" Neither one of them replied. Before anyone could speak again, the doorbell rang. "I'll get it." Valerie said, standing from the couch and exiting the room.

Carlotta moved towards me, reaching her hand out towards mine. "Don't touch me." I said, pulling away from her. "Valerie may have her own fucked up reasons for lying to me, but you? It's all you've ever done."

"Valerie was very clear that I needed to stay away from you."

"You lied. You made me feel terrible for not telling you the truth about our daughter, and you knew all along." I said, a lump rising in my throat.

"I needed you to stay away from me."

"I covered for you!" I shouted. "You are the one who caused the accident, and I let you go. You manipulated me, like you always have."

"There's a lot more to it than that, Jackson. I thought you were Valerie, leaving the house. I thought I was following her, that she was going to tell the police that I killed Charles."

"Save your bullshit excuses." I snarled. "Get the fuck out of my house."

"Fuck you, Jackson." She said, venom in her voice. "You always want to play the victim, but you're no angel. I have made a lot of mistakes, but you are far from perfect, whether you killed Charles or not."

I ignored what she said, pushing past her and making my way to the bathroom. Locking the door behind me, I opened the medicine cabinet and removed the small orange bottle of Hydrocodone once more. I shut the cabinet, staring at myself in the mirror for a long moment.

Tears spilling from my eyes, I opened the bottle of pills and shook one into the palm of my hand. I set the pill on the counter and grabbed a small glass cup from next to the sink. Using the bottom of the cup, I crushed the pill, and then leaned forward to snort the powder.

I splashed my face with cold water and wiped the counter clean. I opened the bathroom door and made my way back into the foyer, with every intention of going upstairs. However, as I made my way past the living room, I saw them. Valerie and Carlotta stood, uncomfortably, as they faced two people sitting on opposite ends of the sofa in front of them.

Our mother, and Austin's boyfriend.

"What the hell is this?" I asked, making my way into the room. Our mother turned to me, a crooked smile etched across her face.

"I caught this one lurking outside, thought Valerie might want to have a word with him." Our mother said. She looked tired, with dark bags beneath her eyes. Her skin was dull, a stark contrast to her usual glow. It seemed as if, somehow, she'd lost weight since the last time I'd seen her.

I looked to Valerie for the first time since entering the room. Her eyes were swollen and red. She stood, rigidly, as she stared intently at the young man on the couch in front of her. Billy (or was it Graham?) sat uncomfortably on the edge of the couch, his body facing almost the complete opposite direction of our mother next to him.

"How do you know my son?" Valerie asked, breaking the silence.

"We met at a concert." He said, not looking up at her. Valerie and I made eye contact for the first time.

"Do you love him?" She asked, her voice firm but gentle.

"Yes." He replied.

"Why did you lie about your name?" He didn't answer. His eyes were directed intently at the ground. "Well?" She continued, after a moment.

"I don't know how to explain." He said, his voice quiet.

"Start by telling us your real name." Valerie said.

"It's Graham. Graham Ryan."

"So what is it you don't know how to explain?" She asked.

"I met Austin, because I was supposed to meet Austin." He replied, finally looking up from the ground.

"What does that mean?" I asked.

"It means that someone told me to become Austin's friend. I never had any idea that it would become something more than that."

"Someone *told* you to be Austin's friend?" Valerie asked, a look of confusion on her face.

"Yes". He replied. "I love him, though. I swear."

"Why would someone want you to be friends with Austin?" Our mother asked, her eyes locked on Graham.

"To get information about his father." At this, Valerie let out a sob and collapsed into the chair behind her. "That fucking bastard." She cried, in between sobs.

"I want you to know that I love Austin. I really, really do." He paused, as he began crying. "I was supposed to be his friend but I wasn't supposed to fall in love with him. I did, though. I love him, I swear to you." He wiped his face with the sleeve of his shirt, and returned his focus to the ground in front of him.

"Who was it?" Valerie asked, finally.

"I can't tell you that."

"What the fuck do you mean?" Valerie said, springing from her chair and stopping barely an inch from Graham's face. I moved, quickly, placing my arm between them. "Val." I said. She backed up several steps.

"I just can't tell you who. You won't understand, but I just can't." He said, as he began fumbling for something in his pocket. He removed a small slip of paper. "But I can give you this."

I took the paper from him and unfolded it. Written in pen across the small scrap of paper was an address. "What is this?"

"Go there." He said. "Tomorrow, at 5pm, they'll be there. I don't know where Austin is, I swear to you, but I think you might find answers there."

"How do I know this isn't a trap?" I asked.

"I guess you don't." He said. "But that is all I have to offer."

"You can go now." Valerie said, after several seconds.

"What?" I replied. "Val, are you sure?"

"Either he's telling the truth, and may have just handed us the answers we've been looking for." She said, turning from him. "Or he was sent here to convince us to walk into a trap. Either way, he has nothing more to offer us."

Graham stood from the couch and began making his way out of the living room. As he reached the foyer, he turned and spoke once more. "If there's anything else that I can do to help, I'm here." He turned and left, the front door closing behind him several seconds later.

Our mother stood from the couch, bracing herself firmly on the arm of the sofa. She made her way to the sidebar, grabbing it for support as she reached it. She poured herself a drink and turned towards us. "So, who is going to go?"

"We should send the police." Valerie said.

"The police are not on your side." Our mother replied. We both looked at her, surprised.

"What do you mean?" Valerie asked.

"Whatever this is, whatever it is that Charles was involved in." She said, taking a sip of her drink. "It's very dangerous, and I think the police are involved."

"What are you talking about?" Valerie asked, shocked. "There's something not right about that Detective Lewis". Our mother replied.

"I said the same thing!" I exclaimed, almost shouting.

"There are too many things that don't add up." Our mother replied.

"So what do we do?" Valerie asked.

"I'll go." I said, firmly.

"If you go, I'm coming with you." Valerie replied, looking at me. There was fear in her eyes.

"I'll go with you." Carlotta said, speaking for the first time since Graham had arrived. I had almost forgotten that she was there.

"Absolutely not." I snapped.

"There's strength in numbers." She replied. "He's my nephew too."

"It's fine." Valerie cut in.

Before any of us could reply, the sound of shattering glass pierced the silence. Our mother had dropped her drink. "Mother!" I exclaimed. "Are you okay?" She didn't reply. She looked at me, her eyes focused but fearful. She reached out to brace herself on the sidebar, her hand just missing the polished mahogany as she collapsed onto the floor.

CHAPTER SEVENTEEN: Love of Life

Our mother lay in her hospital bed, her head resting on two stiff-looking pillows. Since arriving at the hospital nearly two hours beforehand, she had regained consciousness only twice, just long enough to ask for a cigarette. "No mom, no more cigarettes." Valerie had said. "We'll see about that." Our mother quipped back with a devilish smile, before drifting off to sleep once more.

Eventually, the glass door slid open and the doctor returned, adamantly reviewing the paperwork on the clipboard in front of him. "Well?" I asked, exchanging a glance with Valerie. The doctor slid the stool from underneath the lab station and seated himself upon it, in-between Valerie and me. "The tests came back normal." He began. "Or, as normal as to be expected."

"Then why did she collapse?" Valerie asked.

"My guess would be exhaustion. Her body is very, very weak."

"How weak?" I asked, my eyes locked on my mother. Even in her sleep, she seemed tired.

"I told her several weeks ago when she decided to stop treatment that—"

"When she did what?" Valerie replied, her voice thin and tired.

"I apologize. I assumed that you knew."

"How long does she have?" I asked, my eyes unwavering from my mother.

"I'll be completely honest with you." The doctor began, pausing to adjust himself in his seat. "I would be surprised if she leaves the hospital." Valerie stood from her chair and moved closer to me, taking my hand in hers. "Thank you for being honest with us." She said. "Could we have some time?"

"Of course." The doctor said, standing from his seat. "We are lessening her sedation. She will still be medicated to ease any pain she may be feeling, but hopefully she will regain consciousness soon." He made his way out of the room with a slight nod and an earnest smile. Valerie and I sat in the same position for several moments, not speaking until there was a soft knock on the door.

"I brought food." Carlotta said, entering the room. She placed two large paper bags on the small table near the room's only window. "Any update?" I stood from my chair and moved towards her, throwing my arms around her and burying my head in her shoulder, crying. "Jacky, what is it?"

"This is it." Valerie replied.
"I'm so sorry" Carlotta said, rubbing her hand reassuringly on my back. "I need a minute." I said, pulling away from her and moving towards the door. As I left the room, Valerie moved to follow me. "I'll go." I heard Carlotta say. "You stay with her."

I reached the waiting room, collapsing onto the stiff sofa near the elevator. My body was numb, my mind racing. Approaching me from behind, Carlotta placed her hand on my shoulder. "I'm here for you, Jacky." She said, softly. "You may not want to talk to me right now, but I'm here."

"Could literally anything else go wrong?" I said, with an uproarious laugh. "I mean, fuck." Carlotta chuckled, moving to stand in front of me. "We've always had a talent for living the most supremely fucked up lives." She looked down at me, with a tender smile. She reached out, wiping the tears from my cheeks with her hand.

"I never even thought I would care if she died." I said. "In fact, I actually used to hope that she would."

"She's a complicated woman." Carlotta replied.

"There's an understatement." I said, chuckling.

"It's okay for you to not know how you feel." She said.

"I'm trying to keep it together for Valerie." I said. "I'm not good at it. I've always been the one in crisis."

"She's glad to have you here. I know she is." I knew Carlotta and Valerie had probably never spoken about any such thing but, nevertheless, her words were comforting. "I'm going to use the bathroom, will you be okay here for a second?" She asked.

"I'll be fine." I said, giving her a faint smile. She turned, making her way down the narrow hallway off of the waiting area, following the small sign labeled "Restrooms". Several seconds later, a familiar voice spoke out.

"Hi." She said. I turned, to see Jules standing in the doorway leading to a row of hospital rooms, my mother's included. I stood from the couch, turning to face her completely.

"Jules." I said. "It's good to see you."

"I saw your mother's name come across the monitors." She said, moving towards me to embrace in a hug. "I'm so sorry."

"Thank you." I replied.

"I know maybe you don't want to see me right now." She said. "But I wanted to let you know that I am here for you."

"I haven't been avoiding you." I replied. "There's just a lot going on."

"I wouldn't blame you if you had been." She said.

"I'm far from a perfect person, Jules." I said, exhaling. "I've told plenty of lies."

"A relationship shouldn't be founded on lies, though"

"I can't really think about any of that right now."

"I understand."

"I appreciate the kindness that you've shown me." I said. "I value that." She didn't reply, instead moving in to kiss me, lightly, on the cheek.

"Ah." Carlotta's voice rang out from behind us. "This must be Jules." I hadn't heard her return to the waiting room.

"Julianne Ryan" Jules said, reaching out to shake Carlotta's hand. "And who might you be?""

"Carlotta." She replied, her lips curling into a devilish smile. Jules dropped her hand.

"As in…" She began.

"The one and only." Carlotta replied, cutting her off.

"Well, it's very nice to meet you." Jules said.

"Thank you."

"So, what's going on with your mom?" Jules asked, clearly looking to change the subject.

"It's not good." I replied. "She's very sick."

"I know you two don't have a very good relationship." Jules said. "But I'm sure this is very difficult for you."

"Profound." Carlotta scoffed.

"I'm sorry." Jules started. "Do you have a problem with me?"

"I'm quite protective of Jackson." Carlotta began. "He's no angel himself, but he has a tendency to let other people hurt him. Myself included." Jules didn't have a chance to reply, however, as the doors to the waiting room swung open, and in walked Detective Lewis.

"Mr. Arrington." He said, his voice scruffy and unemotional. "I was hoping I might find you here."

"What can I do for you, officer?"

"Detective." He reminded me. "Is your sister here as well?"

"What is this about?" Carlotta interjected.

"I would like to have a word with you and your sister, Mr. Arrington."

"Fine." I said. "Come with me, then." Jules reached out to grab my hand. "I'll catch up with you later." I said. I moved away from them, towards the hallway leading to my mother's room. "Carlotta." I said, turning and motioning for her to follow me.

Detective Lewis and Carlotta entered the room behind me, and I slid the glass door closed behind them. Valerie, still sitting next to our mother's bed, looked up at us. "What's going on?"

"I've come to discuss some developments in the case." Detective Lewis began. "Of your husband's murder."

"What kind of developments?" I asked.

"Are you sure you don't want to have this conversation in private?" He asked, nodding towards Carlotta."

"Just tell us whatever it is you came to say." Valerie said, her tone short.

"All right then." He said, exhaling. "We no longer believe that your son was kidnapped."

"What are you talking about?" I asked, incredulously.

"We have reason to believe that your son is the one who murdered your husband." Detective Lewis started. "And that he is now on the run."

"That is ludicrous." Valerie shouted. "What kind of evidence?"

"I'm not at liberty to discuss all of the details of the investigation with you." He began. "But I can tell you that a handkerchief covered in your husband's blood was found in your son's possessions."

"No, this is a mistake." Valerie cried.

"I'm telling you this as a courtesy, Mrs. Sinclair" He said. "Before the story is made public."

"That doesn't even make any sense." I interjected. "I was drugged! I saw someone in the room."

"As I've told you before" Detective Lewis started. "There is no substantial evidence to prove that there was ever a third party involved."

"Are you fucking kidding me?" I spat. "So what, I drugged myself?"

"You do have a history of substance abuse, no?"

"How dare you."

"People have done crazier things for family, Mr. Arrington."

There was a stir from our mother's hospital bed. She blinked several times, wrapping her frail hand around the rail of the bed. "Valerie?" She muttered, her voice barely audible.

"Thank you for the information." Valerie said. "We will have to discuss this further at a later time. Our lawyer will be in touch."

"Are you sure?" Detective Lewis replied.

"I'll show you out." Carlotta interjected, motioning towards the door. Detective Lewis gave a nod, and with that, they exited the room.

Our mother continued waking, slowly, her eyes moving back and forth between the two of us. "Hi Mom." Valerie said, softly.

"Hi." She replied, her voice weak.

"Are you in pain?" I asked, moving into the empty chair next to her bed.

"No. They have me on the good stuff." She chuckled. "I just want a fucking cigarette."
We laughed, Valerie reaching out to take my hand in hers. "I'm not going to make some grand apology, if that's what you're expecting." Our mother began.

"We don't have to do this, mom." I said.

"I am sorry." She said. There were tears in her eyes. "I wasn't a very good mother."

"It's okay." I replied, my voice cracking slightly.

"I don't believe in regrets." She said, pausing to let out a light cough. "I don't regret the choices I made in my life, but I feel remorse for the ways that they affected the two of you."

"We will be okay." Valerie said, stroking our mother's hand.

"Thank you, Valerie." Our mother said. "For stepping up for your brother, in all the ways I didn't."

"That's what family's for, no?" Valerie replied.

"And Jackson." She said, her eyes locking with mine. "You are very smart, and very capable. Let go of the past, of me. Accept your role in your own failures, and move on. You deserve to be happy."

"Okay, Mom." I said, as I began to cry.

"And don't have a fucking funeral for me." She said. "Cremate me, do whatever you want with the ashes, but no funeral."

"Okay. Whatever you want."

"I love you both." She said, as she drifted into unconsciousness once more.

Valerie and I stayed vigil at her bedside for what felt like hours. I rested my head on her shoulder, our hands tightly interlocked. Eventually, the line on the monitor went flat.

A kind nurse entered the room, offering her condolences as she draped a sheet over our mother. Valerie and I exited the room, standing in the hallway as another nurse entered the room, closing the door and drawing the curtain behind her. Valerie embraced me, tightly, in a hug.

"I'll take care of everything here." She whispered. "Can you check on Madeleine?"

"Are you sure?" I asked. "I can handle this, if you want to go home."

"Go take care of your daughter, Jackson." She said, with a smile.

"I love you." I said, leaning in to kiss her on the cheek. "Let me know when you're coming home."

"I love you, too." She replied, as I turned to exit the hallway. I made my way into the waiting room, down the narrow hallway and to the restroom. I pushed open the door, sliding the lock into place behind me. I made my way to the sink, propping myself up on the counter with my arms as I let out a sob.

Fumbling in my pocket, I removed a bottle of pills. Unscrewing the lid, I placed two in my hand. I turned on the faucet, cupping water into my hand, and with one gulp, swallowed both pills.

I left the bathroom, taking the elevator to the main floor of the hospital. As I reached the lobby, I exited the elevator and headed towards the large revolving doors that led to the street. As I approached the doors, however, a familiar face caught my eye.

Aunt Charlene.

I made a beeline towards her. "Charlene." I called out. She pretended not to hear me, scurrying hurriedly through the lobby. "Charlene!" I yelled. Finally, she turned towards me.

"Jackson!" She said. "What a surprise. What are you doing here?"

"I could ask the same of you." I replied. She hesitated, eyeing me carefully.

"I'm here for a doctors appointment, dear." She cooed, finally.

"Are you living in New York now?" I asked.

"I am not." She replied.

"Well, you don't seem sick."

"I'm sorry?"

"Who makes a doctors appointment out of town?" I asked.

"I'm here on an extended trip, things come up." She said, coolly. "I don't owe you an explanation regarding my medical appointments."

"I know you're up to something." I shot back. "I don't have time for this."

"You're making something out of nothing." She said. "Can't a woman visit a doctor without such questioning?"

"I have to go now." I replied, making my way towards the doors once more.

"It's always a pleasure to see you."

"Oh, and if you give a fuck." I began. "Your sister just died."

"I'm sorry to hear that –" She started, but I had already turned to exit the building.

I waited outside, tucked into an alleyway near the entrance to the hospital. After nearly 45 minutes, Charlene finally exited the hospital, taking a right and making her way down the sidewalk. I followed her, carefully, maintaining enough distance to keep her from noticing me.

Eventually, she stepped into an alleyway that led behind the hospital. I watched, hidden near the entrance to the alley, as she stood, waiting near one of the hospital's employee entrances. Finally, the door swung open. A woman exited the hospital, a scarf tied tightly around her neck - she was draped in a black coat, her hair pulled up into a hat. Her back was to me.

"Took you long enough." Charlene quipped.

"I'm having second thoughts about some of this." The female voice replied. The voice was distant, but familiar.

"Oh, stop it." Charlene replied. Suddenly, the other woman's phone rang loudly from within her purse. "Fuck." She exclaimed, startled. She fumbled through her purse, looking for her phone. Eventually, she removed it, though it slipped from her hand, landing with a thud on the hard concrete. She bent over to retrieve it, and as she did her coat rose slightly in the back, revealing a small tattoo.

Of a rose.

CHAPTER EIGHTEEN: The Secret Storm

The ride home was nothing more than a blur, the driver trying, and failing, several times to start a conversation. It was almost as if we were moving in slow motion, my heart pounding in my chest, my breathing short and rapid. Thoughts were flying through my mind at a thousand miles per hour, my hands were clammy and damp with sweat.

"Are you okay, Mr. Arrington?" The driver asked.

"Yes." I managed to mutter, though my voice was short and forced. Somehow it felt as if the car were getting smaller. I fumbled for the small switch on the door of the car, the window quickly disappearing into the frame of the door as I pressed it. I leaned towards the window, the cold air slashing against my face as we sped through the streets of Manhattan.

I remembered waking up in Jules apartment, confused, her gentle voice reassuring me that I was okay. I remembered as she cried, as she told me the story of her brother. I remembered her shirt rising ever so slightly, to reveal a tattoo of a small rose on her lower back.

As the car pulled up outside of the house, I threw the door open before we had even come to a complete stop. Forcing myself from the car, I collapsed onto the sidewalk, the concrete scraping the palms of my hands as I fell. My breathing had grown increasingly short and rapid. There was a sharp pressure spreading across my chest.

"Jackson!" I heard Valerie's voice call out. "Jackson!" Her footsteps grew louder and louder, and before I knew it she was kneeling next to me, cupping my face in her hands. "What happened? What's wrong?!" I let out a loud sob as the tears came. Valerie stayed next to me, gently caressing my back as I fought to catch my breath.

"It's all right." She whispered, leaning in to kiss me on the back of my head. "Tell me what happened." I stood from the ground, wiping my face as I turned to look at her.

"It's bad, Val." I said.

"What is it?"

We made our way inside as I filled her in on what I had seen and overheard. Her face was still and emotionless, but her eyes were wide with horror. "What are we going to do?" She asked, her voice quivering.

Before I could answer her, I noticed Madeleine standing at the top of the stairs, just peering out from around the corner. "Madeleine, sweetie." I began, making my way up the stairs. "I'm so sorry I didn't come home to check on you." I wrapped her in a tight hug.
"It's okay." She said, pouting as she looked up at me.

"I love you." I said, kissing her forehead.

"Uncle Jackson." She started. "You were crying." I looked down at her and couldn't help it as the tears came back to my eyes.

"I'm okay." I said stroking her cheek.

"Were you crying about my dad?" I didn't know how to respond. "Were you crying about Austin?"

"I'm worried about him, is all."

"Do you think he's okay?" She asked.

"I sure hope so."

"Someone at school said that you're my Dad." I felt my heart sink, my mind going completely blank.

"Charles was your Dad, sweetie."

"They said you're my *real* dad."

"There's no such thing as that." I said. "Where you came from doesn't change who your family is. Charles loved you very much, you were his daughter."

"Wasn't he bad?" She asked, her face scrunched in confusion.

"People who do bad things still love people." Valerie said, making her way up the steps.

"Is Austin still my brother?"

"Of course he is!" She said, embracing Madeleine in a hug. "Your family is still your family, always. I know everything is changing and that's probably very confusing for you, but you will always have a family that loves you."

"You have the best mom in the world." I said.

"Madeleine, I need you to go to your room, sweetie." Valerie started. "We can talk about this more later, but I need to talk to Uncle Jackson now, about adult stuff." Madeleine gave us both a hug and a kiss on the cheek before making her way down the hall and to her room.

Valerie and I returned downstairs and made our way into the living room. I immediately poured myself a drink. "Jesus Christ, Jackson." Valerie said, not far behind me. "Is this really the time to be drinking?" I ignored her, swallowing the contents of the glass in one swig.

"We need to be very careful about what we do next." I said.

"What did you have in mind?" She asked, skeptically.

"We have to go to that address."

"You think that's where Austin is?" She replied.

"At the very least, it's where Charlene and Jules are."

"Carlotta will be here any minute." Valerie said. "She insists that she's coming with us."

"That's fine. We'll fill her in when she gets here."

"Okay." Valerie said, almost as if she was trying to convince herself.

"I'm going to go to the bathroom, splash some water on my face." I said, making my way out of the room before she could respond. I quickly closed the bathroom door behind me, throwing the medicine cabinet open and scrambling for the bottle of pills. I poured three into my hand and washed them down with a swig of water, and then I crushed up another and snorted the powder from the countertop.

When I returned to the living room, I found that Carlotta had arrived. "Valerie told me everything." She said. How long had I been in the bathroom?

"We have to go." I said.

I sat in the backseat of Valerie's SUV, once again staring aimlessly at the buildings whizzing past. Carlotta turned to look at me from the passenger seat, though I avoided making eye contact with her. Valerie hadn't said a word since we'd left the house.

"I will beat both of their asses if I have to." Carlotta said, attempting to lighten the mood. Neither of us replied.

Eventually we arrived at the address Graham had given us, a small house nestled in a quiet neighborhood in upstate New York. We sat, parked just around the corner from the driveway, for what felt like hours, though, in my state of mind it could have been minutes. Finally, just before 5 PM, a car pulled up.

Charlene stepped out of the car and approached the house, fumbling with the keys as she unlocked the front door. Several moments later, another car arrived, rolling to a stop as it entered the driveway. The driver door swung open, and out emerged Jules.

"Fuck." I muttered.

After Jules had entered the house, closing the door behind her, Valerie spoke for the first time. "So what the fuck do we do now?"

"We go in after them." Carlotta replied. "And we get Austin."

"What if he's not in there?" I exclaimed, my voice louder than intended. "That will only make things worse."

"We don't exactly have a lot of options here." Valerie said, softly.

We exited the car and approached the house cautiously. As we reached the front porch, I made my way to the window, peering through the small opening in the curtains. The house was dark. Valerie turned the handle of the front door but, as to be expected, it was locked.

"How are we going to get in?" Valerie asked.

Before I could reply, Carlotta called out from the opposite side of the porch. "Come here!" She hissed, her voice a loud whisper. She was standing next to a window. "It's open." She said, motioning at the window, which was in fact, ever so slightly ajar.

"I'll go." Valerie said.

"No, let me do it." I replied.

"He's my son."

Gently, Valerie slid her hands underneath the window and pushed until it moved upwards. She shot us a quick look before disappearing into the house.

"This is a bad idea." I whispered to Carlotta. "These people are dangerous."

"She's going to be fine." Carlotta assured me. Sure enough, several seconds later, the front door opened, slowly. On the other side, stood Valerie. We entered the house, closing the door carefully behind us. "I can't see shit." Carlotta whispered.

We tip toed our way through the small front hall and into the equally small kitchen located adjacent to it. There were voices coming from upstairs, one of which definitely belonged to a man.

"What the fuck are we going to do if they come down here?" I asked.

"Cross that bridge when we get to it." Valerie replied.

"I think our main priority needs to be getting in there." Carlotta said, pointing to a metal door on the opposite side of the room. It was locked, from the outside, with a heavy padlock.

"What do you think is in there?" Valerie asked, her voice laden with fear.

"There's only one way to find out." Carlotta replied.

"And how do you suggest we break the lock without being heard?" I replied, frantically. Carlotta moved towards the door, removing a bobby pin from her hair as she did. "You really think that's going to work?"

"I learned how to hot wire a car when I was 15 years old. You think I can't pick a lock?" She said, seriously. "Come over here and shine your phone light."

I did as she said and, sure enough, the lock popped open several seconds later. "We clearly aren't dealing with experienced criminals here." She scoffed. She pulled open the door, revealing a dimly lit staircase into a basement.

"I'll go first." Valerie said, moving past both of us as she began making her way stealthily down the stairs. Carlotta and I followed, cautious of each footstep as we descended into the basement. The stairs led into a relatively small room, with beige walls and carpet to match. A small, outdated television sat perched atop an empty bookshelf, next to which were a refrigerator and microwave. In the corner was a small bathroom - its light flickering on and off aimlessly. On the opposite side of the room was a small, twin-sized bed. In it, lay Austin.

"Austin!" Valerie exclaimed, rushing across the room and collapsing onto the bed, throwing herself on him. "Oh my God!" She whimpered, between sobs.

"Mom?" Austin questioned, his voice ripe with disbelief. "Holy shit." He collapsed in her arms, tears forming in his own eyes. Carlotta grabbed my hand, squeezing it gently, a smile on her face.

Finally, Austin stood from the bed, our eyes locking for the first time. "Uncle Jackson!" He exclaimed, moving towards me and wrapping his arms around me in a firm hug. "I can't believe you're here." We stayed like this for a long moment, there were tears streaming down my cheeks.

"Are you okay? Did they hurt you?" Valerie asked.

"I'm fine." Austin began. "Nobody hurt me."

"We have been worried sick about you." Valerie said, grasping his hand. "I'm so sorry, baby. I'm so, so sorry."

"It's okay, Mom." He said, smiling softly.

"You were hurt. You had surgery. Are you okay? Are you still hurting?"

"They gave me medicine, for the pain."

"You need to see a doctor." I interjected.

"I was mostly just worried they were never going to let me go." Austin said, catching himself as he began to choke up. "They kept telling me I was leaving, but that I wasn't going home."

"Who is they, Austin?"

"There were two women, but I only really ever saw one." He replied.

"How old?"

"50's? 60's maybe?" He said. "There was also a man."

"What did he look like?" I asked.

"I never saw him, but I heard his voice upstairs a lot." He trailed off. "Who are you?" He asked, noticing Carlotta for the first time. She didn't reply.

"This is your Aunt." Valerie began. "Carlotta."

"My father's sister?" Austin asked, hesitantly.

"Yes." Carlotta replied.

"What are you doing here?" He asked, his tone growing defensive.

"I'm sorry for all the damage my brother did to you." Carlotta said, earnestly.

"She has been a big help, Austin." Valerie replied.

"It's nice to meet you, I guess." Austin said, his eyes darting towards me. "Thank you."

"I know you don't know me, Austin." Carlotta began. "But I am very, very glad that you're okay."

Austin didn't have a chance to reply, however, as a voice rang out behind us. "Well, what a beautiful family moment." Charlene said, making her way down the stairs. Jules was not far behind. "Heartwarming, really."

"It's over, Charlene." Valerie hissed. "You're done."

"Oh, my dear, sweet girl." Charlene replied, with a chuckle. "It's only just begun."

"What is that supposed to mean?" She asked.

"I have to say, I'm surprised you got this far." Charlene quipped. "I didn't think any of you had it in you."

"I never should have trusted you." I hissed, my gaze locked firmly on Jules. "My mother was right about you."

"Don't make this about me, Jackson." Jules replied, coolly. "And don't make it about yourself."

"You lied to me about your dead brother." I screamed. "You're sick."

"Why do you think I did all of this?" She snapped. "Everything I told you about my brother was true."

"You left out the part about being a kidnapper and, if I'm to assume, at the very least, an accessory to murder."

"So sanctimonious you've gotten." She quipped. "Was I this judgmental when you passed out drunk at a bar full of strangers? Or when you got behind the wheel and almost killed your nephew?"

"You used me, and your dead brother, to get revenge. That makes you just as bad as Charles."

"You were never supposed to be a part of this, son." Charlene interjected. "You simply showed up at the wrong time, and set it all in motion."

"Don't you fucking call me that." I shouted. "And what is that supposed to mean?"

"You stumbled into town and provided the perfect line of communication into that house. You were the perfect pawn, for both of us, against Charles."

"What possible reason could you have to want Charles dead?" Valerie asked. "You met him exactly one time in our entire marriage."

"Oh, Valerie." Charlene replied with an uproarious laugh. "I knew Charles well before you did."

"What are you talking about?" Valerie replied, stunned.

"As I'm sure you know, Charles studied abroad in London during his senior year." Charlene began.

"During that time, he interned at the company I worked for."

"You're lying." Valerie hissed.

"He was one of the best young salesmen I'd ever seen." She started. "There was something almost sinister to him, the way he enjoyed duping people into things that were never going to benefit them in the long run."

"A piece of shit from the start." Austin seethed.

"There was only one person who could mentor him to his full potential, and that, of course, was me." Charlene said, with a smile.

"What does that mean?" Valerie asked.

"I won't say that Charles didn't try to seduce me. He tried to seduce everyone." She laughed. "But I taught him everything he knew."

"He never once mentioned anything about you." Valerie shot back.

"Well I imagine it would've been difficult for him to explain that I was the reason two of you met."

"You're so full of shit!" Valerie shouted.

"Charles came from a mediocre family, of which he was deeply ashamed. He was looking for someone to create a life with, someone that came from the *right* family." Valerie didn't reply. "The party that you met at? Tell me, Valerie, who do you think told him to go?"

"You used me."

"I gave Charles the tools he needed." Charlene replied. "Unfortunately for you, you take the bait."

"You are a special kind of monster." Valerie said, her eyes filling with tears.

"I'm a woman who knows how to make things happen."

"Get to the point." I interjected. "If Charles was so dear to you, why would you want him dead?"

"Charles was never supposed to die." She replied. "That part stemmed from you."

"Excuse me?"

"See, I had known that Charles and Julianne were sleeping together for some time. I assumed she was just one of his usual mindless flings, but she was always lurking, always nervous and distant. It didn't take me long to figure out what she was up to."

"Plotting a murder?" Carlotta quipped.

"Plotting revenge." Jules said.

"And what better way for the both of us to get revenge, than to work together." Charlene said.

"You still haven't said you would want to hurt him." Valerie replied.

"I don't think you'd understand even if I did, dear." Charlene began. "Let's just say, he got a little too big for his britches and, as it turned out, he was loyal only to himself. Not even I was safe."

"And exactly how does that make it my fault that he's dead?" I asked.

"We were there to confront him." Jules began, stepping forward, towards us. "It was all supposed to end then. Charlene was going to get her money, and Charles was going to go to jail."

"So what changed?" Carlotta asked.

"He kept telling us to keep our voices down." Jules started. "Said the two of you were drunk, that you'd just stumbled up to bed a few minutes beforehand."

"Turns out he was right." Charlene interrupted.

"What are you talking about?"

"You came stumbling down the stairs, drunk out of your mind and high on who knows what." Charlene said, an almost empathetic tone in her voice. "It was really rather pathetic."

"You started ranting and raving incoherently about how much you hated Charles." Jules began. "About what a loser he was, how you were going to get him away from your sister. You were so fucked up you barely realized we were there."

"Surprisingly to no one, he snapped." Charlene said. "Grabbed you by the throat and shoved you into the wall. He might've killed you, if Julianne hadn't stopped him."

"Stopped him how?"

"By killing him, of course."

"For whatever it's worth, Jackson." Jules began. "I did us both a favor."

"Yeah, except now the police are coming after my son." Valerie shot back.

"What?!" Austin exclaimed.

"I have to take credit for that one." Said Charlene. "He was just asking too many questions."

"Because of Graham." I interrupted.

"Who is Graham?" Austin asked, confused.

"Billy." I began. "His real name is Graham. And he's Jules' brother." The room went silent.

"How did you know that?" Jules asked.

"He told us that someone told him to befriend Austin, and his real name. He just so happens to have the same last name as you. What are the chances?"

"What do you mean someone made him be my friend?"

"That was all it was ever supposed to be. I had no idea it would be something more." Jules said, her voice suddenly soft.

"Regardless of that." Valerie interjected. "You were just going to send a minor to prison for murder? Your own nephew, at that?"

"Please. He's a teenaged white boy in America, he'll never spend more than 6 months behind bars." Charlene replied, smiling smugly.

"You're not going to get away with this." Valerie said.

"Luckily they've got a little help." Detective Lewis' voice echoed out as he made his way down the stairs.

"I fucking knew it." I said, as he reached the bottom of the steps. "You god damn scum bag."

"I can't particularly say I blame you for that opinion." Detective Lewis scoffed.

"What is in this for you?" Valerie asked, wiping tears from her eyes. "What could possibly make this worth it?"

"Money." He replied with a laugh. "And after all, Charlene here is an old friend of mine. As was Charles, of course."

"You're a real psychopath Charlene, you know that?" I said, venom in my voice. "You never bothered to have a god damn thing to do with your family, yet here you are ruining all of our lives."

"For what it's worth, I always kept tabs on you. Disappointing as they may be." She retorted. "I'm going to let you handle the rest of this, Detective. Come Julianne, let's go." Charlene and Julianne began making their way up the stairs. I darted in their direction, trying to stop them, but Detective Lewis stepped in front of me, flashing his gun.

"I wouldn't do that if I were you." He snarled.

"Fuck you." Valerie shouted. "You are a sick, disgusting person."

"I've been called worse."

"What are you going to do?" Carlotta asked. "Kill us?"

"Of course not." He replied. "I'm going to arrest you for harboring a fugitive." He said, nodding towards Austin.

"Harboring him at a house that none of us have ever been to before?" Valerie shot back.

"A house in your deceased husbands name, Mrs. Sinclair." Detecitve Lewis replied, smugly.

"How can you do this to somebody's family?" Valerie said.

"I don't give a fuck about your family." Valerie didn't reply. Instead, she spat in his face. Before I knew what was happening, he lunged at her, wrapping his hands around her neck. They tumbled to the floor, his knee pinning her to the ground. She choked and spat, gasping for air.

I lunged at him, trying my hardest to pull him off of her. He threw me backwards, sending me crashing through a glass coffee table. Austin attacked him, grabbing onto his hair and wrestling as hard as he could. Detective Lewis managed to throw Austin from his back. His grip tightened around Valerie's neck. I scrambled, trying my best to crawl towards them as I watched the life leave my sister's eyes.

Suddenly, there was a loud, cracking thud. Detective Lewis' grip loosened as he toppled over, collapsing on the ground. There was a large gash on the back of his head, bleeding profusely. Above him stood Carlotta, a tire-iron grasped firmly in her hands.

Austin and I made our way towards Valerie, who was still gasping for air. With our help, she sat up. "What happened?" She asked.

"He's dead." Carlotta said, her voice frail and thin. I looked up at her, kneeling next to Detective Lewis' lifeless body, her fingers on his neck.

"What do we do now?" I asked.

"We get rid of the body." She replied.

CHAPTER NINETEEN: Where the Heart Is

Days turned into weeks and before I knew it, two months had passed since that night. Things began happening at such an accelerated rate that I often find myself lying in bed at night for hours, trying to make some sense of what life had become over the past year. So far, no luck.

After Detective Lewis' "disappearance", a new detective stepped in to resume the responsibility of solving Charles' murder. Detective Andrew Bailey, a middle aged man with an uneven haircut and ill-groomed facial hair, somehow made Detective Lewis seem a ray of sunshine.

"Why don't you tell me what really happened that night?" He had asked, his tone firm and void of emotion.

"I've told you a dozen times." I replied.

"You expect me to believe that your nephew, a murder suspect and fugitive, miraculously returned home on the same night Detective Lewis disappeared?"

"The two have nothing to do with each other."

"I beg to differ."

"You're bluffing." I replied, calmly. "You haven't made an arrest. You have nothing."

The fear that he did, in fact, have something lived constantly in the back of my mind. The fear that he was in on the plan to frame Austin consumed me. Since returning home, Austin had retreated into himself. He spent most of his time alone, though even when he was around Valerie and me, he was far from his normal self. Valerie herself had become distant and agitated, as to be expected.

On this particular day I sat in my bed, mindlessly scrolling through my phone. I glanced at the clock: 3:43 PM. Somehow three hours had passed since the last time I had looked at the time. I swung my legs over the edge of the bed and stood, stretching and groaning as my bones cracked, loudly.

I made my way down the hallway, towards the staircase. As I walked past Austin's room I heard a series of subdued coughs. I stopped, knocking on the door. "It's me." I called out. "Come in." He replied. When I entered the room, he was perched near the large bay window, which was ajar. He lit the bowl in his hand and exhaled the smoke out of the window.

"Everything okay?" I asked, shutting the door behind me.

"Is that even a serious question?" He asked, with a slight chuckle. I pulled up a chair next to him.

"Let me have a hit of that." I said, motioning for the bowl. He passed it to me. I lit it, inhaling sharply and holding my breath for several seconds. Finally, I exhaled.

"Shit's really fucked up, huh?" I said, laughing.

"There's an understatement."

"We're gonna be okay, kid." I said, giving him a light punch on the shoulder.

"You don't know that." He replied, his gaze focused out the window.

"You're not wrong."

"You know Mom still hasn't said a word to me about Bil--Graham." He said, correcting himself. "About me being..." He drifted off.

"She loves you. She doesn't care."

"Not enough to say something, anything."

"I don't think she knows what to say." I assured him.

"She's my mother." He quipped. "She should think of something." I reached out, taking his hand in mind and giving it a gentle squeeze. He turned to look at me. "I think I'm going to jail."

"That's never going to happen." I said. "Never." He didn't have a chance to answer, however, before there was another knock at the door. He scrambled, grabbing the bowl and the weed, quickly stashing it in the drawer of his nightstand. "Come in!" He shouted, awkwardly. The door swung open and in entered Valerie, followed by Carlotta.

"What's wrong?" I asked, instantly standing from my chair.

"Jackson, I need you to stay calm." Valerie began. "Okay?" Carlotta stood several steps behind her, with tears in her eyes.

"What is it?" I asked.

"I am going to turn myself into the police." She replied.

"What are you talking about?" Austin asked, his voice cracking.

"I am going to confess to killing Charles, and Detective Lewis."

"Valerie what the fuck are you talking about?" I asked, stunned. "You didn't kill either of them."

"They found Detective Lewis' body, Jackson." She began. "It washed up late last night." My heart dropped from my chest.

"That doesn't mean you confess to killing them." Austin replied. He was crying now.

"My DNA is under his fingernails." Valerie said, avoiding making eye contact with Austin.

"We'll get you a lawyer. A good one." I pleaded.

"They're going to come for Austin, and try to take me down with him." She said, softly. "I'm going to go to them first, and tell them it was all me. That I hid Austin away because I knew he was a suspect, and that I killed Detective Lewis when he came after us."

"You can't do this." I said, moving towards her. "Please, Val. I can't do this without you."

"You have to." She said, touching my cheek. "You have to take care of my family. Our family."

"I am the least qualified person on earth for that job."

"Jackson, you are a good person." She replied, pausing to wipe away her own tears. "I am so proud of you, and how far you've come. You are going to be okay."

"You can't just decide to do this, Valerie." I said, hysterically. "You can't just leave us."

"I have always taken care of you, haven't I?" She asked. "That's what I'm doing now, Jackson. Always. But this time I need you to take care of my family, for me. Carlotta is going to help you."

"What are you talking about?" I asked, looking at Carlotta.

"I want to do this with you, Jacky." She said, moving towards me and grabbing my hand. "We are going to be okay."

"No, no, no." I said, pulling back. "This can't happen. This is not realistic."

"You don't have to do this." Austin interjected. "I'll turn myself in. I'll say I did it."

"You will do no such thing." Valerie shot back, cutting him off. "Absolutely out of the question."

"So now I just have no parents?" Austin asked, wiping away the tears from his cheeks.

"You will always have me." Valerie said, wrapping her arms around him. "I will always, always be with you." They stayed like this for a long moment.

"I've set aside what money is still accessible." Valerie began, pulling back from Austin. "I've had everything transferred into your name."

"I don't know how to do any of this." I replied.

"There's more." She said. "Mother left you everything."

"You're lying."

"I'm not."

"Why the fuck would she do that?"

"Because she loved you." Valerie said, moving towards me and kissing me softly on the cheek. "Jackson, you all need to leave the country."

"What? No!" Austin objected. "We'll never see you."

"You don't need to see me regularly." Valerie said, stroking his cheek lightly. "Not like that."

"I can give them a better life here, somewhere I know." I replied, exasperated.

"This is going to be a media nightmare, and you're a celebrity." She said.

"Maybe 20 years ago." I scoffed.

"You have to take them somewhere they can have some semblance of a normal life."

"Okay." I replied after several seconds, looking up at her.

"Would you mind grabbing Madeleine?" She asked. "I'd like to have some time alone with my kids."

I brought Madeleine from her room to Austin's, Carlotta pulling the door closed behind us as we left. Without a word, we made our way to my bedroom. She crawled into bed with me, nestling her head on my shoulder as we lay there, crying. Eventually, she drifted off to sleep. I moved, slowly, standing from the bed and entering the bathroom, scrambling in the dark for my little orange bottle of pills.

CHAPTER TWENTY: Generations

It had been over a month now since Valerie had turned herself in. Over a month since we had left everything we knew behind, since we had picked up and moved across the Atlantic to start a new life in England. Things were going about as well as one would expect. That is to say, things were not great.

We arrived in the middle of the night, tired and uneasy from hours on the plane. The driver of the cab had dropped us off in front of a large cottage, nestled in the woods not far from the city. A home that Valerie and Charles had purchased, but never visited together.

Madeleine spent most nights crying for her parents, and Austin rarely appeared from his room. At times it felt like Carlotta was the only one holding it together, though even she seemed distant and afraid at times.

On this particular day, we sat at a park not far from where we lived. Carlotta and I were seated next to each other at a picnic table, finishing up the last of the lunches we'd brought. Not far from us sat Austin, nestled under a tree, his nose buried in a book. Madeleine played excitedly with children she had just met, as if they'd been friends forever.

"I'm worried about them." I said, keeping my voice low to make sure Austin didn't overhear.

"I am too." Carlotta replied. "But we're going to be okay."

"I don't know how to do this." I said. "I don't know how to fix things for them."

"You can't fix things, Jackson." She said, grabbing my hand. "You just have to help them heal." Just then, Austin glanced over at me, our eyes locking. He flashed me a brief smile before returning his attention to the book in front of him.

"I'm afraid I'm going to make them worse."

"They had a criminal father and their mother is in prison." Carlotta said, laughing. "You'd have to drop the ball pretty hard."

"Thank you." I replied, chuckling. "Thank you for everything."

"Whatever this is, whatever we are or might be." She began. "I'll always care about you, and besides, they're my family."

"I am sorry that things happened the way they did." I said.

"I know." She replied.
My attention shifted towards Madeleine. Watching her laugh and shout, surrounded by other kids, brought a sense of comfort to my mind, which was otherwise racing at a mile a minute. Before long, my thoughts consumed me. Thoughts of worry, of fear, of love, for these children that I knew I now had to protect.

I barely heard as a notification pinged on Carlotta's phone. Removing it from her pocket, she unlocked the phone and began reading, her brow furrowed with worry. "Holy shit." She said. "Jackson." She turned the phone towards me. Across the top of the screen in large, bold font, was a headline:

"MURDERER ON THE LOOSE? VALERIE SINCLAIR ESCAPES POLICE CUSTODY."

I barely had time to process what I had read, however, as something else had caught my attention. Across the open field in front of us, just past where Austin sat and Madeleine played, there was a woman sitting on a bench. Her face was encompassed by a scarf wrapped tightly around her head, her eyes shielded by large, round sunglasses. Nevertheless, it was a face I recognized.

Charlene.

Next to her sat a man. A man who looked a lot...like Charles.

TO BE CONTINUED.

Made in the USA
Columbia, SC
30 June 2020